I0557290

IDIOT

DEAR KAMI

A NOVEL BY

HOLLY SMITH

AN IMPRINT OF LITTLE PORTLAND PRESS

COVER DESIGNED BY
COVERSBYCHRISTIAN.COM

Don't stay where you are tolerated. Go where you are celebrated. -Author Unknown

Holly Smith is an animal lover, wife, mom (human and animal mom), writer, and lover of nature. She loves to write, read, cook, ride horses, garden, draw, and laugh.

Holly has an American Cream Draft Horse, an Appaloosa, and a Gypsy Vanner. She loves all three. She also has an indoor potbelly pig named Amelia.

She lives in the PNW where it's so majestic, writers and artists alike, travel unknown distances to rest and visit the very town she calls home.

Current and Relevant Societal Subjects Covered:

-mass school shooting

-drug use

-sexuality (LGBTQ)

-anxiety, panic attacks

-relationships

-first job

-college

-abuse

-foster care/adoption

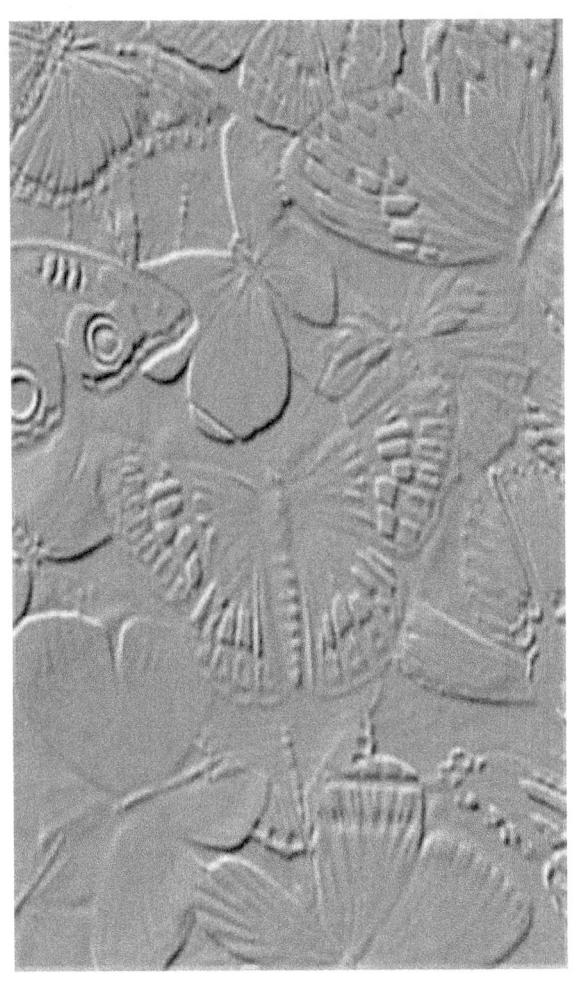

Dear Kami,

My so-called therapist thinks it will be helpful for me to jot down good and not-so-good memories about growing up. She thinks it will help me understand why I've made certain choices in my life. *She* thinks . . . *She* has no idea!

I bet she was raised in a big ole two-story-house with a swing on the front porch, white picket fence, a bunch of brothers and sisters, and a mom who woke her up every morning for breakfast before school. I bet she had an upstairs bedroom where she would smell bacon cooking in the kitchen. I bet her dad kissed her on the forehead before he left for work each morning. What does *she* know about me? What does she know about my life? What does she know about having absolutely nothing or no one? Nothing!

This is a bunch of crap! She sits in her expensive office chair with her expensive college degrees hanging on the wall and *suggests* I may be depressed, or angry, or both.

WTF!

I wish everyone would *stop* focusing on me and pay attention to people who want it. I am sick of therapists, counselors, social workers, and basically everyone.

I mean . . . How many times can I say the same thing? No one *really* listens. I am starting to think they ask, ask, ask with the hope I may say something that contradicts something I've already said. I don't lie. I hate liars. Ray lies. Mama told me once you get a reputation for lying, you never shake it.

The therapist says I should write to you because you're the person I know and trust most. How ironic! I am sure you will share that sentiment.

So, here goes, Kami . . .

I am going to *try* to write and focus instead of focusing on her three-inch-long, bright pink fingernails with sparkles on the ends.

Still distracted . . . It looks like she's wearing a two or three carat diamond ring. I bet it's real. I see the Coach purse she tossed under her desk like trash, just like the rich kids in school. Their parents buy them purses and bags the price of cars, and cars the price of a small house. Oh, what I could do with the money she threw away buying a bag she obviously cares nothing about! Indulged brats always make me ill. On one hand, I feel sorry because they live so blindly, and on the other, I feel like poking salt in their eyes because they're rude, undeserving, and walk through life without really seeing anything. *What* can this lady tell me about love, loss, being invisible, and living in hell? Nothing I don't already know!

I'm trying here . . . Trying to get the nail polish, posh clothing, expensive jewelry, and ridiculously expensive luxury bag out of my mind...

Finally! I'm able to concentrate and am no longer doodling in the margins.

So, here goes with my first crappy memory. I wish I could forget Ray!

"Hey Idiot! Get over here!"

I looked over my shoulder, hung the bucket on a rusty nail in the old fence, and walked to the cabin.

"Hurry up!" Ray shouted. "I ain't got all damn day to wait for you."

I hurried.

"What're you feedin' them damn chickens?"

"The feed Mama made."

"What did *I* tell you about feedin' them

damn chickens?"

I looked at the dirty wrinkles circling his seething mouth and eyes.

"Didn't I tell you that stuff is a damn waste of money and they only get it once a week? Didn't I?"

I nodded. Of course I nodded. I was too scared to do anything else. Too scared to talk.

"What? Did you say something, Idiot?"

"Yes, sir," I whispered. "But when Mama left for work this morning she said—".

"She said," he mocked. "Again, with that shit. *I* do the tellin' around here, not her, not you, not nobody else. Them chickens can eat bugs and whatever else they can find. I ever catch you feeding that stuff to them again I'll beat your ass till you can't sit for a week. You understand me?"

I trembled, "Yes."

He raised his hand, put his fingers on my forehead and roared, "What?!"

Afraid of being hit, I murmured, "Yes, sir.

I'm sorry. Yes, sir." I was about to cry and didn't want him to see me do it.

His hand fell to his side and I relaxed. "That's better." He shook his head as he stepped into the cabin mumbling, "Damn, stupid idiot."

My thoughts were fuzzy and stumbled onto you. I wondered what you were doing. I couldn't find you anywhere. I walked down to the creek to see if you were there. I needed you.

"Kami?" I called. "Kami, where are you? Can you come out and play today?"

Feeling sad, I sat down by the creek and played with the doll I made from sticks and yarn. "Hey Susie, have *you* seen Kami? I bet you have. She should teach you to draw like she taught *me* to draw."

You showed up with the cool wind that often twisted and curled up the creek wearing the sparkly crown I always admired.

I swung my head around and squealed, "Where have you been? Do you want to play? Susie wants you to teach her how to draw like you did me. No? Oh, you wanna read instead? That's okay. I snuck the book Mama got me out of the chicken coop. We can read it together. You can go first if you want to."

You read to Susie.

We sat on the creek bank talking, laughing, and gossiping, until you shispered, "Shhh. Do you hear that? It sounds like yelling."

"Yeah," I said. "Mama must be home. I better get back."

I returned Susie back to the safety of the oak tree hollow before I left.

I could hear him hollering and got scared. *I hope he doesn't hurt Mama again. I don't like to see her sad. I hope he doesn't see me. He'll beat me if he does. I have to sneak close and be very quiet.* I sidled up below the house and peered in through the window. Mama and Ray were standing in the kitchen.

"No, please," Mama was saying. "Please, Ray! I didn't mean nothin' by it. I just--".

"You just *what*?" Ray shouted, spit spewing from his tightly curled lips.

"I just thought feedin' the chickens would make Eva happy. She likes feedin' them chickens."

"Make her happy? What do I care about her bein' happy--and what've I told you about

14

callin' her by that name? She's a goddamned idiot, and she needs to know it. If I catch you callin' her that *one more time* you're gonna wish you woulda listened to me. You understand? And you don't do no tellin' round here. I'm the man. Both of you do what *I* say. I don't wanna hear nothin' else about you tellin' her anythin' again. If you think she should do somethin' you check with me first. Ya hear me?"

Mama sobbed. "Oh Ray. She ain't no idiot. She's learnin' real good." As soon as the words were out I knew they were a mistake.

"Don't you backtalk me woman! Who the hell you think you are?" Ray hit Mama and sent her stumbling back onto the stovetop. "Nex' time you backtalk me it'll be worse. Now get dinner fixed. I don't want no excuses. An' next time you're in town, I need more whiskey!"

Ray grabbed a half-empty bottle, stomped into the living room, and plopped down on the old couch sending dust and dirt whooshing into the air when he did.

I waited until Ray was asleep and snuck into the house; I didn't want to get caught.

"Mama, oh Mama!" I whispered. She was sitting at the kitchen table, her head on her arms.

"Shhh, baby girl."

"Are you alright?"

"Yeah sweet baby girl."

"You don't look alright. I'll get you a wet rag."

"No, Eva. He might wake up an' I don't want him hearin' ya. Go back outside till dark. Once he's goodn' passed out, I'll come get ya."

"Okay, Mama."

I snuck back out avoiding the squeaky porch boards, and ran to the old chicken coop. I snaked my body through the small opening and sat with my knees to my chest on the cold dirt floor listening for Mama and talking to the chickens. "Hey, Ruby Sue and Opal. Ray's at it again. He hit Mama pretty bad this time. I don' know why he keeps hittin' her. Kami says he's kin to the devil. He might be. Wouldn't surprise me. She calls him Demon."

I ran my hands over their soft backs. "Thanks for lettin' me come in here with you. I like to sit and pet your feathers. You're so soft. I wish I was soft like you instead of being cut up, bruised, and dirty. You and all your sisters are lucky not to have to live in the house with Ray. I

16

wish I could live out here with you, except I'd be afraid I couldn't take care of Mama. I like knowing when she needs me. I can hear her from the creek, but not so good from here."

The rain was slow and dribbled through the cracks in the coop, making pools in the dirt floor where the chickens liked to dust bathe. I fell asleep in the straw, curled on my side, with Ruby Sue under one arm and Opal at my heart.

Once Ray was drunk, sleeping, and it was dark, Mama knew the rain would block sounds she made leaving the house. Her soft knock woke me.

"He's asleep," she whispered. "He won't wake neither. He never wakes when it rains. Come on to the house. I'll get ya fed and we'll read."

"I'm glad you're okay, Mama." I crawled out of the coop and stood, stretching my stiff body. "I was worried about you. Kami says Ray *has* to be kin to the devil."

"Maybe so. He used to be so nice. I . . . I don't know what happened ta him."

"Kami calls him Demon."

"Kami's a smart girl." She held the door open for me and said quietly, "Go ahead to the bedroom. I'll fix ya some soup. It's vegetable, 'cause we don't have no meat."

I scampered into the bedroom and curled up to wait. A few minutes later, Mama came in with a steaming bowl of soup.

"I love you so much, Princess. I don't like ta see ya cry when . . . when Ray . . . ya know."

"Oh, Mama! I love you too! I wish we could leave here and live somewhere else."

"Don't say that baby. We got a roof over our heads and food ta eat. I know it's rough sometimes, but life's rough. I jus' wanna make sure ya can read and write so ya can getcha a decent job one day and can pay yer bills."

When I finish my soup, I ask, "Why does Ray hate me so bad? I've never done anything to him."

"Oh, my Princess. He don't hate ya. He's just a damn drunk. Thas' all. Just a damn drunk. He probably ain't never gonna change neither. He don't think he's doin' nothin' wrong."

"When he hits you, he doesn't think he's doing anything wrong?"

"No, He don't. I…I shouldn' push 'em like I do. I argue, and it makes 'em mad."

I curled up in bed with my favorite raggedy old blanket that smelled like Mama's cigarettes. "I love you Mama. Thanks for the soup. It was delicious. What kind of job do think I can get when I'm older?"

"Well Princess, I always thought you'd make a purdy bank teller. All those bank tellers are purdy just like ya is, ya know. You're smart enough for it too. Thas' why I been teachin' ya ta count money. Ya could work in a grocery store if ya wanted, like me. It's a good job. It ain't always fun, but I get payed good. Enough of this talk. Let's get focused on your books."

Later,

Eva

Dear Kami,

What you don't know is that was the first of many troubling memories I scribed in my journals over the years.

I have a new school counselor now. I like her much better than the last one. Her name is Melissa. She was adopted when she was a baby and doesn't know her birth parents. She said she used to wonder about them, but the adoption was closed, so it was difficult to track anyone down. That somehow makes me like her more. It's like she has her own pain and her own struggles. She says she doesn't wonder about them anymore though.

I'm different. I'd love to know my father. I am nothing like Ray, thank God! Mama said she had a one-night stand with a guy named Travis. That's about all she remembers. That and the fact he had black curly hair and was just passing through on his way to visit friends and family. I often wonder if he knows he has family he left behind. I used to love playing *What If* with you.

What if Travis had known about me and had fought for me and Mama? What if he'd loved me and protected me? What if we'd lived in a nice house in the country and had horses? I've always wanted to have horses. I used to dream of getting a baby horse for Christmas and naming it Bug. That will never happen though! That's why *what-ifs* are dangerous. They get your hopes up. And for what? A big fat nothing . . .

In my weekly sessions with Melissa, we talk about a lot of things. Mostly about change. She wants me to start writing in my journal about Mama and Ray again, but I told her I just don't have the words for the drama anymore. That's when she suggested I write in my journal and continue to address each entry to you because we were best friends growing up and shared so many secrets.

I hadn't written in my journal in years and cringed at the thought of seeing the old entries again. There are probably five or six in all, and I haven't read anything from them in forever. I started writing in them because my first therapist made that my homework, so I did it.

I stopped when one of the kids who lived with me in a foster home read what I wrote and made fun of me. She not only made fun of *what* I wrote but also *how* I wrote. That devastated me.

It took every ounce of strength and stubbornness I could muster not to destroy all of them after that. But there were things I knew I would want to remember later, so I hid them out of sight instead, hoping they would also be out of mind. In every foster home I bounced in and out of, I hid them under the floorboards or under the mattress in whatever shared bedroom I slept in.

Melissa says change comes through hard and sometimes dirty work. She wants to help me be authentic. I hope I can find the strength to forgive Ray. I don't want to carry around this resentment forever. I won't forgive him for him, but so I can make some changes for me. I *have* been thinking about the early years a lot lately.

So, back to reading and writing I go, I suppose:

Ray hated me before he ever really knew me. On the farm that freezing day, I knew he wanted it to happen. He had a wild look in his eyes—crazy wild, like a demon-- and I knew.

"Hey Idiot!" he growled. "Get over here! What in the hell'r ya doin' over there? You ain't readin' that damn book again, is ya?"

I stuttered, "N—no sir. I ain't," I lied, trying to hide the book behind my back.

He grabbed my arm above my elbow, spun me around and grabbed the book Mama had given me. He snarled, "You lyin' lil' Idiot! Take y'er clothes off and give 'em here! Now! Then you get back ta choppin' and stackin' the firewood like you was s'pose ta be doin' in the first place." His eyes were darting around like a madman's and his upper lip curled up as he laughed. "You wanna hide stuff and be a li'l liar, then ya can work without no clothes. Ya won't have nowhere to hide them damn books naked. Ya sure a scraggly, scrawny, dirty li'l thang, ain't ya. Stupid, scrawny, and dirty."

I could feel my body going numb, so I swung the axe as fast and as hard as I could, trying to warm up. I also felt something wet tickling my thighs. I assumed I was sweating although I was freezing. It wasn't long before Ray noticed and came flailing out of the house like a tornado. His eyes were still darting around madly, and he didn't make eye contact. Instead, he stared at blood from what ended up being my first period smearing between my thighs.

"Blood? You're fuckin' bleedin'? Didn't yer Mama teach ya about those things? You nasty li'l Idiot! Ya can't do nothin' right, can ya?" I was too afraid to move and too afraid to cry.

"Serves ya right! Yer Mama can deal with this mess when she gits home. Keep on workin.' A little blood ain't no reason ta stop. Anything that bleeds fer seven days and don't die is jus' . . . Jus' aint to be trusted!"

His glare made me cringe inside. He snarled his upper lip again and had an evil twinkle in his eye.

In that moment, I felt the most unrelenting humiliation I'd ever felt in my life like it was throwing me to the ground and refusing to let go. My chest felt tight and I felt paralyzing terror. This would be the first of many panic attacks to come.

I knew things were only going to get worse when Mama got back home.

And they did. He started drinking and didn't quit until sometime much later.

Looks like I have a visitor, so I will write more later.

Ta-ta,

Eva

Dear Kami,

We'll fast forward the last few hours and pretend they never happened. I *wish* they never happened! I *will not* ingest the disgusting blobs of garbage they try to feed me here. Everything is slopped together on a tray. All I can think of when I see and smell the junk they call food is, *Looks and smells like the rotting slop Ray used to throw out to the chickens.* So, I turn into a mouth-breather as soon as the trays are distributed. I carefully move food around on my plate, so it looks like I've eaten more than I really have. They monitor what you eat, though, I have to choke down some of it. What I can't spit out in my napkin ends up being puked up and flushed down the metal toilet attached to the cement block wall in my blue padded room.

I hate meals around this freak show. I guess this is what happens when you spend too much time only *thinking* about killing yourself and not going through with it. I've told all of the therapists and other people in this God-forsaken joint that I would have jumped that day if I really wanted to end it all at that actual moment.

It's my life and I'll end it when and how I want!

Not being actively suicidal sure makes these other freaks seem like the *real* nuts. I mean, yes, I have a means, mode, and plan, but damn it, *that* wasn't *the* day it was supposed to happen for me.

Having been thrown in and out of these freak shows over the years enables me to *help* the psychs. I've got the lingo down. Not that it's a good thing . . . But, it *is* amusing, and helps pass the time.

At least I didn't botch my own death this time. These freaks all failed, and that's why they're here. One girl took too many pills, but not enough; another sliced her wrist, but only superficially; this other dude shot himself but lived through it. That's why jumping is the perfect way to end an unwanted life. Jumping from umpteen feet in the air, pretty much guarantees that I'd end up flat as a pancake, especially with me weighing over 110 pounds.

Earlier in the day I was committed to this joke of a nut ward, I remember sitting breathing in the cool air and looking down on the living dead walking through the streets. They were asleep. They were robotic. They were depressed. I felt an urgent calling to end this life, no matter what. This world is a free-for-all I'm no longer willing to be part of. I've been thinking about suicide since I first tried and failed (like these other freaks).

As I sat with my legs dangling down from a billboard ledge, people passed by, seemingly with no concern for or care about my existence. Their disregard for me made me feel eerily alone. More than usual. I sat wondering how people come to the decision to off themselves. I think about that a lot. Do most people wake up and think, *I think I'll kill myself today?* I doubt it.

I sat there most afternoons. The first time I climbed up there I was nervous, but by this point all I felt was numb. People probably looked up and thought, *There's that weird girl with black hair, and black clothes, who never talks.* That's me, I guess. The weird girl.

I went there for silence, fresh air, and the hope I might find a reason to talk myself out of jumping, or for some reason to stop feeling insignificant.

I leaned back on one elbow and inhaled deeply, choking back deep drags with each toke. I could feel the THC taking over my shoulders and neck. Next, I was acutely aware of the rise and fall of my chest and slowed breathing.

It was a great way to wrap up a shitty day and a shitty life . . . until my mouth started feeling drier than the Sahara Desert. The dreaded cottonmouth had struck, and I was its captive. My eyes were also starting to feel dry. I reached up and massaged them for what felt like ten minutes. When I opened them again, I squinted and realized the neighborhood assholes were making their way over, undoubtedly to climb my billboard.

WHAT.

THE.

HELL.

I carefully began my descent down-- when I end up killing myself, it is certainly not going to look like an accident. I was thirsty. I never climb up with water, because when you think about killing yourself, you don't tend to care about drinking water. So, I slurped what seemed like gallons of water from a city park drinking fountain until I was satisfied I wasn't going to dry up and wither away.

Predictably, I was trapped in a haze of lethargy, so I decided to head to the foster home, although I wasn't looking forward to the excitement I would inevitably face there.

At home, I lay under my bed on the floor, wrapped in a blanket and thought about how you and I used to spend countless moments on the creek bed drawing and playing *What If*. When I could manage to sneak away, I would grab Susie and wait for you. We never drew anything fancy, we just liked spending time together. Oh, how I miss spending time with you on the creek bank!

And that's when it happened. My foster mom knocked on the door, found me laying under the bed, and walked in with the social worker. They repeatedly asked if I was high and asked about the phoned-in reports about me attempting to jump off of a billboard. But, that wasn't *all* they wanted to know.

As if I weren't already some huge weird outcast in the eyes of most of the *normal* kids and *perfect* adults, now I was *really* in the spotlight. As someone who would rat on their friends . . . On their *only* friend . . .

But I *had* to do it. I had to. I need to keep telling myself that. How could I not? Mama's words kept circling through my head, "Always do what's right, baby. It ain't right ta hurt nobody."

I was already on the guidance counselor's radar because of my previous suicide attempt, so frequent visits were not only expected, they were pretty much routine. Melissa made sure I understood that I never needed an appointment to talk with her which was perfect because otherwise, I would have probably chickened out. I sheepishly meandered into her office, sat in her chair, and waited for her to return. I couldn't sit still and was almost in tears. I was also sweating, which is something I rarely do.

Once Melissa came back and had time to fully digest what I was telling her, she kept repeating, "Eva, this isn't a joke. Are you *sure* about Ian's plans? This is serious, you know!" Then, she adjusted her clothing, cleared her throat, and apologized for the questions.

"Look, I believe you. But, this is very serious, and I need to act swiftly and accordingly. You have no idea how proud I am of you, but I need to get some things moving. I am going to ask Mr. Peterson to come in so you can also share this information with him. I know you are not comfortable around many people, but I will help you through it. I promise. I am so sorry you're going through this, but I am so happy you made the right decision."

And that was the day I foiled Ian's plan to conduct a mass school shooting. That was the day I ratted on my *only* friend and the guy I lost my virginity to. That was the day I progressed from weird goth girl to super freak. Melissa called me a hero, but instead, I felt like people looked at me like I had leprosy.

Ian and I had shared so many secrets. The police couldn't get enough of me. I hate the police. The last time I saw a police officer was the last time I spoke to Mama. I had to get away.

Fuck my life!

Thankfully I left when I did that day, because I heard the assholes who climbed up my billboard as I was coming down were all arrested for the possession of marijuana. Whew, at least I dodged *that* bullet!

Although I denied being high, once I was in the hospital for observation, they tested me for drugs. *So much for that foster home!* I violated the *only* rule they really had: don't do drugs.

It was a decent placement, but I just never really clicked with them. I guess being sixteen with seven placements under my belt makes some people a little leery about bringing me into their home.

I'm not a difficult kid, in retrospect. I don't punch holes in walls or doors, don't set things on fire, am not sexually promiscuous (I've only done it with Ian, and I didn't even like it), and I don't sneak out of the house very often.

I like being on the floor *under* my bed by no later than 8:00 p.m. My only issues are my dislike of typical conversational crap, my affinity for weed, and the fact that I am obsessed with my own death.

Lights out around this joint is at 10:00 p.m., so I will have to write more tomorrow. Staff here are pretty strict about the curfew.

Until tomorrow,

Eva

Dear Kami,

I don't know if I should say good *morning* or just "hi," because it *hasn't* been a good morning. In fact, it has been one of the shittiest mornings I've ever had.

What's wrong? (I'm laughing out loud right now).

Oh, nothing. Just the fact that Melissa met with one of the shrinks here, and she told her I'm not being very cooperative. She also said I'm manipulative.

Melissa gets upset when she thinks I'm not cooperating. I also know she doesn't think much of people who try to be manipulative because I heard her call Hailey O'Hannan a manipulative little brat under her breath a few weeks ago.

I don't want her to stop liking me. She's really the only person who is nice to me anymore. I mean *really* nice. She's real. I hate all of these posers walking around pretending to be nice when all they really see is my black, sometimes dirty hair and my dark makeup and clothes, and immediately dislike and judge me.

I know the difference between someone looking *at* me and someone looking *through* me. I'm *not* an alien, a robot, or other foreign thing warranting a crude visual dissection.

I'm a person . . .

With feelings . . .

And a whole lot of fucked up . . .

Auggghhh . . . Melissa said I have to be agreeable and at least try if I want to keep working with her. She wants me to work with everyone while I'm here although she understands I don't feel comfortable around most male doctors. I just feel more comfortable around women. Melissa says it's not a *bad* thing. She says it's part of what makes me unique.

She and the other psychs think I'm angry. They believe I get angry when I'm criticized and have a hard time forgiving people.

If Melissa wants me to focus my anger on Ray, I'll focus on Ray.

I'm beginning to think I'll never be allowed to forget what he looks like . . . Forget what he

sounds like . . .. Forget what he smells like . . .
Forget what he feels like . . .

FML.

I'll do it though. I'll start where I left off and write more about the Demon. Gaaahhh! I hate him!

. . . He started drinking and didn't quit until sometime much later, when he passed out.

He woke up before Mama got home, though, and as soon as she walked through the screen door, he met her face with an already bloodied fist. He had been punching the walls and had knocked several new holes in the wall beside the stove in the kitchen. Now, he met Mama's face with his fist, time after time, until she collapsed on the floor, cradled in a pool of her blood mixed with his.

Before he continued the attack, he stopped, dropped his pants, and pissed on the kitchen floor while he leaned on the door jam for balance. Mama didn't dare make a sound. Most children would have probably been shocked seeing a grown man piss on the floor in the house, but this was something he did fairly regularly. I wasn't shocked. I also didn't try to help Mama; instead, I remained in hiding, watching from nearby.

Ray's dark eyes winced as he started to snap out his drunken fury. "You cheatin' whore!" he hissed. "If you woulda kept your hands off that other man's dick, you wouldn't have this problem with your li'l Idiot. She'd be more like me instead of some other cocksucker. You sure is lucky I put up with you. Most men wouldn't. Speakin' of puttin' up with you . . . You ain't keepin' up with your womanly duties. You better fix that! You don't want me ta start lookin' 'round ta replace ya with somethin' younger, do ya? I got needs, woman! We both know you real good on ya knees. Don't be bashful now. Hear me?"

That night, I watched from my hiding spot, as Ray took hold of Mama's broken body and repeatedly forced himself in and out while she lay facedown across the rickety old kitchen table. I don't know if I will ever forget the nagging sounds of the table creaking and rocking back and forth muffling the slight, sporadic groans that escaped Mama's swollen lips.

Ray looked up, red-faced and still pushing, slid his hand under Mama's shirt and tugged her nipple, looking straight at me. He grinned and spit, "You wanna piece of this?" His breathing quickly escalated, and he muttered, "You. Like. Whatcha. See. Don'tcha. Li'l. Idiot."

Mama cried out, "Oh Ray! Don--".

My eyes burned and I felt my world going numb as I watched him slap Mama so hard a bruise immediately took shape from black to purple, covering the entire left-hand side of her face. I fled outside.

Later that night, Mama snuck out to the chicken coop to tell me I'd need to sleep there for the night. That was the beginning of the end of my nights spent in the house with Mama and Ray.

That night was the worst sleep I'd ever had. I was angry. It was the first time I'd thought about suicide. I wondered why I woke up day after day just to do it all over again with no end in sight.

ANGRY.

AS.

HELL.

I bit my tongue as I cried to Opal and Ruby Sue and forced myself to swallow the warm, salty blood in my mouth, which wasn't easy to do on an empty, queasy stomach.

Wow . . . It's group therapy time. Woo-friggin'-hoo. . . I *hate* groups! I'm sure I'll be ready to barf after hearing whiny bullshit these morons complain about.

This kid named Frankie is upset because her parents bought her a used Chevy instead of a brand-new BMW like her best friend Kortni's parents bought her. This pre-owned gift apparently sent Frankie into, "Help, I'm going to drown myself mode." Except, everyone knows you can't just drown yourself willy-nilly. Every self-respecting suicide aficionado knows it's human instinct to fight for breath and swim to the surface. So, Frankie apparently held her breath for two minutes, then, swam to the surface in defeat.

Boo-hoo,

Eva

Dear Kami,

Oh, how I wish you were here and could save me from the babbling these time wasters put everyone through! I *hate* group therapy! Oops . . . Said that last time. I'll say it again. I hate it! Used-car cry-baby Frankie wasn't there. Apparently, she's in a padded room somewhere with cameras on her 24/7. Pffish! Are you kidding me?

I got *called out* in group for not participating. WTF? I'm tired . . . Okay??? Is that okay with these full-charging, white-coat wearing, prescription pad-wielding, bunch of in-your-face fanatics? Of course not!

My question is, "Why isn't it okay?" Can't I deal with my own shit on my own time? Melissa says the answer to that question is obvious. She said I'm here because I *don't* deal with my own shit, not that I *can't.*

I didn't ask that question in group. I didn't write or say anything in group, in fact, and that's why my evening privileges have been suspended until I show *meaningful* participation.

FUCK MEANINGFUL!

I'm *not* going to spill my guts in front of a bunch of emotional retards! Not happening!

This place isn't great, but it's not like living with Ray either.

I guess I can handle being here for a while because that's what's going to happen anyway. I'm going to refuse to participate in whiner's therapy, and the white coats will extend my stay-- for my benefit, of course.

After all, they feed us three meals a day, I have a warm bed to sleep in, and I'm not getting hit. The only bad part is that I won't be able to see Melissa if I don't participate.

I'm in a funk! I'm going to eat when they call for dinner and go to sleep early. I hope they put the food on trays and not paper plates. The trays have dividers, so the food doesn't touch. The staff ordered new trays because a guy broke a chunk of plastic off his tray and sharpened it down to a point by scraping it along the rough surface of the concrete blocks lining his room. Needless to say, he tried to slice his wrist using the sharp plastic. At least he didn't try drowning himself! I'll give him points for creativity! *Not!*

The only food I like cooked with everything touching is soup. I basically love every kind of soup. I can't stand it when other kinds of food touch.

It reminds me of the slop Ray used to try to feed the chickens *and me.*

Ray. Ray. Ray . . . Bastard!!!

20 minutes later . . . Dozed off . . .

Dinner bell ringing! Will write more tomorrow. Good night, Kami!

Feelin' funky,

Eva

Good Morning, Kami,

I am still feelin' funky. I must be getting sick from being in this God-forsaken, germy place.

I swear I can *see* germs crawling on the walls and other surfaces despite my impressive cleaning routine. My last foster mom used to say she'd never seen anyone so good at taking "just plain old water and a rag" and making the place spotless. That's all I have to use in here because the white coasts are afraid I'll kill myself with anything more.

This morning, the smell of burnt toast was almost too much to bear. I slid on my paper-thin slippers and shuffled across the concrete floor until I made my way to the metal toilet, screwed to the wall.

I dropped to my knees, and with both hands tightly clutching the rim of the toilet bowl, I appreciated the coolness of the metal and hoped

I wouldn't puke. I was at the mercy of my sour, cramping stomach.

As soon as the nausea disappeared, I grabbed the toast, tore it into small chunks and flushed it. Good riddance!

Once the morning hygiene rush slowed, I knew I'd be called in for my morning session with Dr. Lydia. I usually don't mind talking to Dr. Lydia because she is nice and is easy to talk to. Plus, she's not like ninety years old.

But today I couldn't concentrate. Dr. Lydia said I looked pale and asked about my symptoms. I told her I had none. Apparently, she didn't believe me, because she sent me off to sick call. There, the nurse took my temperature--it was normal. Then she asked *the* question. She asked if I could be pregnant!

I gulped. I couldn't *possibly* be pregnant!

Could I?

I gulped again and replied, "We were careful. We used protection."

My stomach was in knots and was now turning flips. I knew something had to be very wrong. The nurse asked, "What kind of protection did you use?"

I stuttered the word, "C-condoms."

"Well, *that's* a good start! Condoms are great, but they don't always work 100 percent of the time. Are you on birth control at all?"

I could feel my face, neck, and ears turning pink and I cleared my throat and whispered, "No." The nurse was nice. Don't get me wrong.

It's just that I'd never considered the possibility of being pregnant, especially since I never want kids. I'm just not a kid person. I've learned that in the seven foster homes I've been in.

"Okay, dear!" she said, all cheerful. "I am going to need a urine sample so we can do a pregnancy test. It shouldn't take long once we have the sample. Why don't you take this cup and go into the bathroom? Take your time and try to relax. Here's a bottle of water you can sip in case your bladder is empty. If you can't go now, we can try later."

I took the cup and had no trouble filling it to the red line marked on the side.

As I handed over the warm cup I asked, "Will I see Dr. Lydia again today?"

"I doubt it," she said quickly. "Her schedule is pretty tight."

I had too many things on my mind. I was worried Dr. Lydia would find out I lied to her by saying I had no symptoms when she asked. I was also worried I might be pregnant.

I guess I'll have to wait until next week to see Dr. Lydia. When I do, I'll come clean with her. I don't want to get a reputation for lying. Like I said before, Mama always said that is one reputation you can never shake. If I apologize to Dr. Lydia, that should right the wrong since my lie didn't hurt anyone. I hate liars! I don't know what got into me!

The nurse asked me to wait in the lobby while the test was processed. They had every magazine imaginable, but my stomach was having nothing to do with any of that. Instead, I revisited the bathroom-- this time with explosive diarrhea. I feel sorry for the person who cleans bathrooms around this place. That's all I am saying!

The nurse walked out and waved me back behind the nurse's station. Unlike most people I meet, I was unable to read her face.

I held my breath as I waited for my life to change forever. And not in a good way. I've never thought of myself as the mom type, ya know . . .

My heart was beating so hard I could feel the pulse in my head. I reached up to wipe the sweat from my forehead, my hands shaking like I'd just stuck them in an ice bucket.

"Well, Eva, it looks like you dodged a bullet this time," the nurse said, her face serious. You're a very lucky young woman. Raising a child is a difficult task under the best circumstances and is a lifelong commitment. You have so much life ahead of you. I hope you're happy with these results. You seem to have a nasty stomach bug. It should subside in a few days. I will give you something to calm your stomach so you can at least keep fluid down."

For the first time in a *long* time, tears happened.

Yes, they just happened. I didn't expect the crazy rush of emotions that followed the nurse's news. I was wailing and babbling and could not, for the life of me, stop.

I woke to the lingering stench and burning sensation of smelling salt. My eyes and nose were watering. The nurse and Dr. Lydia were on the floor, on each side of me.

As I began to fully awaken, tears streamed down my face. I felt inexplicably calm and told Dr. Lydia I lied to her. I had to. I don't want to be *that* person. A liar . . .

"Shhhh," whispered Dr. Lydia. "You shouldn't talk. Just lie here and rest. We will talk later. For now, just know you have luck on your side; you are a *very* lucky young woman."

"Will I—".

"Ah-ah-ah, you need rest. I'll see you tomorrow at nine o'clock. Until then, rest. I'll call your unit and let them know you need to be on bedrest through the evening," Dr. Lydia interjected.

So you see, Kami, I've had a very busy day. And I *am* tired. I am going to sip this chicken broth and then, I'm sacking out.

Good night,

Eva

Dear Kami,

I *needed* that! What a horrible couple of days! I've never been that sick in my life. These nasty emos are some serious germ carriers. I've watched so many of these people leave the bathroom without washing their hands. I even *heard* a girl *grunting* in the bathroom the other day. I doubt I'll ever forget the stench of her handiwork, because it had a peculiarly strong, sour smell. I was washing my hands and picking the rough cuticles around my fingernails when I watched her walk right past the sink and out the door! I know that's why I got sick! Because of these nasty emos!

Gotta run! Dr. Lydia just called for me.

I'll write more later,

Eva

Dear Kami,

Whoa! Apparently, I dodged the pregnancy bullet, but someone else around my age wasn't so lucky! And she's happy about it! At least that's what Dr. Lydia said. She also said she is proud of me for telling the truth. She isn't mad at me and doesn't think I am a liar. I asked *why* she doesn't consider me a liar and she said, "Because liars don't usually admit their untruths."

I'm good with that!

My session with Dr. Lydia was cut short because of some emergency. Dr. Lydia didn't say what the emergency was, but I just know one of these emos tried something stupid! It may sound mean to call them emos, but that's exactly what they are. Oh, you're wondering what makes me different?

I'll tell you . . .

First of all, one of the girls here is pregnant and is *excited* about it.

Another wants to off herself because her dad slapped her. Sounds like a spoiled brat to me. Ray used to make me cry, but you eventually get used to it. You can get used to anything; trust me. You think you'll die, but you won't. I used to close my eyes and bear the sand and twigs grinding into my skin and mouth while Ray repeatedly smashed me into the dirt, holding me only by my thin hair. I survived. I didn't try to kill myself because Ray got a little rough with me.

The next case is a new boy who is *really* crazy. I almost feel sorry for him. He hears and sees things that don't exist. The other day at dinner, I overheard him telling someone he had a feeling he was being watched and often hears footsteps behind him. Someone asked if he has ever been able to spot anyone following him and he reluctantly said, "No."

Are you convinced yet? If not, I have another case to share. I'm sure it will cement my position.

One of the girls here thinks she is a boy. Yes, she has girl parts, I guess. She was born a girl. She calls herself a transgender. Anyway, that's not the reason I think she's emo. I think she's emo because she has these strange fits. I don't know what else to call them. I'll call her she because I'm not sure what else to call her. Out of the blue, she starts trembling and her heart beats so hard it feels like her chest will explode. She says this feeling rises to her throat and acts like a noose making it hard to breath when this happens. The doctors have ruled out a physical cause and say she suffers from anxiety. Okay, you may be thinking, *so do you* . . . Well, maybe . . .Just not so bad. And, I *deal* with my issues.

Sometimes.

Uggg,

Eva

Dear Kami,

I wish we could magically be nine years old again and draw, laugh, and play *What If*. Well, I'd like to be nine again with just you and Mama. No Ray!

My session with Dr. Lydia wasn't as good as it normally is. I left feeling a little depressed. More than normal. She asked why I don't like participating in group therapy and I told her. Yes, I told her everything! I probably shouldn't have, but I did. She seemed so open before. She told me I am too judgmental and need to think about what makes me react so harshly to the others. She told me not to forget that I am here for a reason.

I really don't feel like dealing with this crap!

First it was Melissa and now it's her. I don't think I ever want to be an adult. Adults have too many weird expectations and rules. But, then again, I don't have to worry about that because I am going to kill myself when the time is right.

She also asked me if she could read my journal. I carry my journal with me everywhere because I *don't* want people reading it. I didn't really give her an answer when she asked, so she asked *again.* Didn't she get the fucking hint? I was kind of shocked when she asked me. Who asks to read someone else's journal? I wouldn't have written half the things I did if I knew someone would ask to read it. I can't let her read the places where I talk about killing myself or the stuff I wrote about her! My only option is to go back and scratch all of those parts out. I guess I could just tell her I scratched them out because I don't want her reading them.

It's raining outside and I am feeling like a nap. Thank goodness for the free time I've earned. I will put it to good use, wink wink.

I'll think of you in my dreams,

Eva

Dear Kami,

Just got called in for group therapy. Wish me luck! I really need this therapy stuff to start going my way or else I'll never see Melissa.

Hangin' in there,

Eva

Dear Kami,

Well, I got held back *after* group today and got singled out *during*. Talk about traumatic!

Dr. Lydia called on me to read an excerpt from my diary.

Why me??? I read three fairly safe sentences.

After group, she said she wanted to keep and read my diary. So, I'm sure I'll have plenty of questions to answer tomorrow. She gave me another notebook so I can keep journaling. Arrghh!

I don't know why she chose *me* to go first. Maybe because I haven't been participating much and she thinks I need to do my part.

The pregnant girl read from her diary too. She really doesn't seem *that* strange. I would be so scared if I were in her shoes, but she seems to somehow be keeping her spirits high.

Maybe I am too judgmental? Maybe I am the emo here!

Maybe I *do* belong,

Eva

Dear Kami,

I don't like writing in this other journal. I wonder if Dr. Lydia will read everything? I hope not!

One of the group therapy rules is not to talk about what happens in group outside the group. I don't think this counts. I hope it doesn't because if writing about group in my journal is against the rules, I'm screwed!

I can't believe pregnant girl, aka Olivia, actually seems normal to me. I wonder what that makes me? We sat together during lunch today and had more in common than I figured. Foster care tends to do that.

Used-car cry-baby Frankie is back, which is great for me because it means the white coats will be too busy chasing down her antics to bother me too much. She seemed more stoic today than normal. Maybe because of the emo meds they have her on???

And there's Molly. She's the girl who wants to kill herself because her dad slapped her once or twice. I really don't like this girl and I have no real reason why. I have a hard time liking people who act like they enjoy feeling sorry for themselves. I always have.

I guess I should be feeling like quite the bitch right now for having these thoughts, but I don't. I'm numb.

Paranoid Billy seems to have taken a turn for the worse. He spent the entire time in group today rocking back and forth. I thought I'd seen a lot of gross shit in my life, but everything pales in comparison to what he did today. Once he seemed satisfied he had utterly mutilated his already stumpy fingernails, he slowly began to pick his nose using the bloody nubs. I thought we would end up suffering through this show the entire time until Dr. Lydia confronted him. It took him eating bloody boogers before she stopped him. Ugghh . . .I've never understood eating fucking boogers! He was sucking his fingers like he was enjoying a really great meal, too.

There's he/she, Harry. I'll be a doll and call her a him because she feels like a he. His real name is Heather, but he wants to be called Harry. He's pretty cool, actually. Olivia invited him over to sit with us at lunch. He has very bad anxiety, but I guess I would too if people attacked me and tried to kill me because they didn't like the way I look or the way I act. He reminds me of Ian.

Oh... Ian... I hope he is okay and forgives me. I hope he finds whatever he is looking for. He really isn't a bad person despite his plan to shoot every bully he came into contact with at La Croix High School. He had a long and detailed list of every person who ever bullied him starting in elementary school. His list included many cheerleaders and jocks. Poor Ian. I miss him!

Thinking of boogers,

Eva

Dear Kami,

I had a surprise visitor today. And soup . . . Melissa came to see me and brought soup. Chicken noodle soup from Chick-fil-A is my fav!

I was so happy to see Melissa! Apparently, she and Dr. Lydia have been in contact about me. I started to cry when I saw her. Until I started sipping my favorite soup, that is . . . My short emotional display surprised me, and I think it surprised Melissa too because she had a shocked look on her face which she quickly suppressed.

I told her about my new friends, Olivia and Harry. She was happy I was making friends and not isolating myself too much which is kind of my M.O.

I talked a little about Ian and asked how and where he was. I could tell it threw her off a bit, although I'm not sure why. After all, we were inseparable. Until I ratted on him . . .

Melissa fidgeted with the buttons on her jacket and finally said, "Look, I know your head is reeling right now. You have been through a lot and I am beyond the moon proud of you. I want you to know that foremost. Ian has a long way to go. He is physically okay but has a lot of suppressed anger to work through. I really don't want to see you go backwards in your progress. You're doing so well. Thinking about Ian is normal and is part of what makes you human. I am afraid any more than a thought, like focusing on him, will just set you back. I want you to continue to focus on getting better. You're such a strong young woman. You deserve to be happy. I know you think that is impossible, but once you learn to embrace happiness, it will not make you feel so uncomfortable."

Silence followed and lingered for what seemed like forever. Melissa broke the awkwardness by clearing her throat and saying, "I need to get back to work but promise to come back and visit as long as you continue to do your best. And I know you will."

I knew the visit couldn't last forever, so I smiled and braced for her to wrap her arms around me. She's a hugger. I don't usually like having people in my personal space, but Melissa never seems to care. I think she hugs everyone whether they like it or not.

Finally, she said, "Keep up the awesome work and I'll see you in a few weeks. I don't want to visit too often because I don't want to impede the great progress you're making."

I knew Melissa was a person of her word and knew I would see her again. It didn't stop my heart from skipping a beat, but I strapped on a smile and told her I'd see her later. I'm not a fan of *good bye* because it sounds so permanent.

Like death . . .

Later,

Eva

Dear Kami,

I felt like I couldn't catch my breath! I kept trying to breathe and the air just stopped at the back of my throat. With my back to the wall, I slid down until I was sitting on the floor with my knees tucked to my chin. I still couldn't breathe! I saw blackness everywhere.

Paranoid Billy shuffled around the corner, swooped past the nurse, and dropped to his knees.

Have I said how much I hate smelling salt? I had the scent of ammonia burned in my nose for days after. Geesh . . . Felt like it burnt my nose hair out. My nose was streaming, and I was exhausted. WTH happened to me?

Apparently, Paranoid Billy caught me as I passed out. I wouldn't have had far to fall because I was sitting on the floor, but I guess I could have ended up with a nice goose egg on the side of my head. That's what the nurse told me anyway.

Billy ran one hand up and down my back and told me to imagine sitting by a fire with a warm cup of hot chocolate. The nurse tried to swoosh him away, but that made him plant himself even more firmly by my side. He wasn't leaving. He knew my pain and he knew it well.

The nurse paged Dr. Lydia. She was in-between patients. Thanks to Billy, I was breathing normally by the time she arrived. She told me I had a classic panic attack.

I was angry, and she knew it. She asked Billy to leave, but he was having none of it. I finally said, "He's fine. He can stay." Then, I let her have it! Yes, I cleared my throat, sat up taller, and said, "How dare you! I trusted you!"

Dr. Lydia stuttered, "I-I don't understand."

I angrily replied, "Molly knows about Ian and what he was planning to do. She told everyone."

"So, you think I told her?" she asked.

I growled, "I know you did! How else would she know?"

Dr. Lydia dropped her face to her hands and shook her head. Her voice cracked, and in an almost whisper, said, "Eva, please. You have to believe me. I did not talk to Molly about you. I would never do that. She must have glanced through your journal when Sandy, my secretary, asked me to step out yesterday. I was only gone for a minute or two."

"That was obviously long enough for her to read part of my journal," I snarled.

"I am so sorry," she replied.

Dr. Lydia asked the nurse to keep an eye on me and was out the door before she could respond.

Billy said, "I don't like Molly. She's mean."

Reluctantly, I admitted, "Billy, I'm mean too. I wrote about you in my journal and called you Paranoid Billy."

"Don't worry about it. Just keep breathing and think about the fireplace and hot chocolate," he replied.

"Is that what you do?" I asked.

"One of the things I do," he nodded.

GTG,

Eva

Dear Kami,

I've made three friends now. Harry saw what Billy did for me and told Olivia, who in turn, invited him to start sitting with us during meals and group.

Yes, I said *us*. I'm part of an us, now, which seems strange. I've never had so many friends at one time. I guess Ian and I were an us, but not really.

After all, it was just the two of us and we never hung out with outsiders. Would have been too weird sine we were having sex, which I never want to have again. It was terrible.

Ian didn't really care for it either, but said he wanted to know what having sex with a girl was like. So, we did it a few times to see if it ever got better. It didn't.

Ian realized he was still attracted to guys and I realized I don't really like dicks. They look like wrinkly aliens when they are soft and are almost scary when they're hard. They get all shiny and reddish. And, the taste . . . Don't get me going! I hated the taste of cock juice and Ian hated the taste of pussy juice. He said not just mine. He thinks they all smell, and he really didn't like all the wrinkles and folds down there. Enough of my babbling about bad sex . . .

I'm just thankful I have friends and that Molly is gone . . .

When Olivia went to the nurse's station for pill call, she overheard them saying Molly was transferred to another ward and they hope she creates less drama over there. Good riddance!

Cry-baby Frankie was the only other person who was normally in our group therapy sessions. I won't call her a friend because I could never have anything in common with her, much less like her. At least her meds finally seem to be dialed in. She's still whiney, but a lot less obnoxious.

Olivia surprised me by stopping by my room a couple of hours ago. She asked about the planned school shooting and if I had a role in it. I expected the questions, of course. People tend to want to know when they're hanging around with someone with such grim plans. I assured her I had no role in the plan and was the one who told, which I'm still not super proud of.

I am happy I prevented people from dying and being shot; I just hated being a snitch.

Olivia started crying when I told her and hugged me. That really set me back. Don't get me wrong, it was fine, I was just shocked. That's all. Her pregnancy hormones must be doing a number on her. That's the only thing I can think of.

With Molly gone, everyone seems more at ease. Billy doesn't pick his nose as often in public and I haven't seen him eat a booger since that time in group.

Harry is not as nervous and has found his funny bone. He has turned into quite the group comedian, which is a far cry from where he started.

Olivia is coming to terms with having another person besides herself to take care of. The idea that having a baby would be all cute, fun, and games seems to have faded.

And, there's me. I have friends. I actually like people and give them a chance to like me back.

TTYL,

Eva

Dear Kami,

The words stupid, idiot, scrawny, and dirty keep ringing in my ears.

I no longer feel numb, and I don't like it. I told Dr. Lydia I don't like it and she said it's normal to feel uncomfortable when you're facing change. Yes, I forgave her. After all, it *was* a mistake.

She says I've been so used to suppressing deep feelings for so long, I'm bound to feel strange when the numbness wears off. I've always struggled with hating the way I look. I guess when you're called names almost daily as a child, it fucks you up a little. And, I'm fucked up! I know I am fucked up.

It's part of what made Ian and my friendship work. We were both reject fuck ups, I suppose. It was a unique bond only we understood. I do wonder how he is doing and I think about him often.

I know I am not stupid though, thanks to Evelyn and Bob. They were the second foster family I was placed with. I believe they truly loved me. They helped me learn how to learn, if that makes sense. They were both retired school teachers and worked tirelessly with me and the one other foster child they had. Her name was Ana. Ana didn't catch on to things as easily as I did though. They said education was the one thing nobody could ever take from you and that it would set us free.

I think I would have been fine if I were able to stay with them. But, they were older and when Bob passed away, Evelyn went downhill fast. Ana and I were placed in other homes and I never heard from her again. She was okay I guess. I was always just so involved in reading and learning new things, I had little time for meaningless things like Barbie's and bullshit.

I don't know how I got lucky enough to have them in my life for four years, but I know I would have had a lot more trouble in school if not for them. I've been thinking a lot about them lately also. I think Mama would have liked them.

I miss Mama. Years after I was taken away, I found out Mama got really bad into drugs. She ran from a drug rehab center and everyone assumed she took to life on the streets. She didn't go back to Ray, I know that much. The social worker said that was the first place they looked for her. They said she had gotten into meth really bad and needed a lot of care. The few teeth Ray didn't knock out of her mouth ended up falling out, so she needed to be somewhere that could handle her medical and dietary issues.

I *look* like talking about dietary issues though . . . I still don't eat food that touches other food on my plate. Except soup, of course.

The first foster family I was sent to live with never really understood me, I don't think. That placement didn't last long because I lost a lot of weight there and was already too skinny to begin with. I know now that eating food out of a trash can isn't normal, but I didn't know it then. I thought everyone did that. Why wouldn't they?

Sometimes Ray wouldn't let Mama and I eat, even though she did all the cooking. When Ray passed out or went to bed, we would scour the trash for scraps of food. There was usually enough for both of us, but when scraps were slim, Mama always let me have them. She said I was still growing and needed them more than she did.

What I wouldn't give to hear her call me Princess again and smell the familiar scent of stale cigarette smoke lingering in her hair. My favorite blanket always smelled like that. I tried smoking a cigarette once and hated it. Ian smoked Marlboro's. I never minded it. I just didn't like to be the one smoking because it made me sick the one time I tried it. Pot excluded.

Anyhoo . . .

Back to my first foster home and losing weight. They didn't like or understand my aversion to having my food touch. They thought I was being a spoiled brat. They would try to force me to eat, which was never very pleasant. One of the other foster kids saw me eating a roll from the trash can and tattled on me. They put a lock on the trash can and said people don't eat out of the trash, dogs do.

The social worker noticed my weight loss and asked the foster parents about it. They tried explaining the situation, but the social worker was furious and said she'd rather have me eating *something* than nothing at all.

In the end, the foster parents didn't really care to have me in their home and told my social worker to find me another placement, which is how I ended up with Evelyn and Bob.

Eating out of the trash wasn't an issue there. Evelyn always fed me at the table with the family, but also carefully placed food items on a paper plate inside the trash can. She knew I snuck the food when no one was looking. I eventually stopped doing that all together after about two years of living with them.

Time for group again,

Eva

Dear Kami,

Group sucked! It was great at first because Frankie was quiet, but that didn't last long. Right in the middle of an unnatural silence, Frankie blurted out something that gave me chills all over. As she spoke, she spat, "Hey Eva, I heard you were going to go all Columbine on your high school. I told my parents and they're mad that I'm stuck in here with an *actual* criminal."

She made everyone very uncomfortable.

Olivia got pissed. Steaming mad. She blurted out, "Are you that fucking stupid? No, she wasn't involved you fucking moron! She stopped, you know, *prevented* a school shooting. And your parents can go fuck themselves!"

"Okay, lets refrain from name calling. Let's stick to the rules and have a civil discussion.

Obviously, the rumor mill here is live and unwell. I am personally going to put a stop to this one. Olivia is correct, Frankie. Eva was not involved," Dr. Lydia asserted.

Suddenly, I broke out in a cold sweat. Billy was there to remind me to think about fire and hot chocolate. He carefully and deliberately rubbed up and down my spine as if he were trying to will me into a state of calm.

The entire debacle upset Harry, who unleashed on Frankie, "See what you've done! You're a bully!" Harry was visibly upset and started trembling. Dr. Lydia quickly worked to calm Harry down while Olivia gave Frankie the I'd love to fuck you up stink-eye.

Olivia is far from what I'd call a yuppie. Frankie, on the other hand... She's all yuppie. Or, at least, she wants to be. Olivia is the type you'd hate to really piss off. She just looks like she'd throw a mean punch!

After all the drama, Dr. Lydia dismissed the group fifteen minutes early.

I was already spent, and little did I know, I'd soon be listening to Olivia spill her guts. She walked in and said, "Hey Eva! I know group was intense. I've got something I really need to talk to someone about though. I keep thinking about it and it's something I can't hold in any longer."

"I understand, I'm okay now. Thanks for sticking up for me back there. Frankie is such a bitch!" I offered.

"I would never *not* stand up for my friends, but now, I need a friend."

So, I told her to have a seat on my bed and I sat Indian style on the rug facing the bed.

And she started . . .

"So, you know I am pregnant. You've never asked about my boyfriend and I've been so thankful for that. I haven't been ready to talk about it until now. Well, you know how I've said I hate my foster parents?

Before I go on, I want to say I hope you don't think I am a bad person."

"You can tell me anything. I am sure I will not think you're bad. I mean, look at me!"

Olivia sighed and said, "You're not a bad person, Eva. Let me keep talking so I don't chicken out and not get this off my chest. I'm telling you this because you were brave and stopped something bad from happening to other people. I need to be brave and do the same."

"Here goes . . .The baby's father is my foster dad. I lost my virginity to him. He said if I told anyone he would say I was lying. I am not his first, and if I don't stop him, I won't be his last."

"How do you know he isn't doing that to anyone now?" I asked.

"I--I don't know. They didn't have any other kids when I left, but it doesn't mean they don't have any now."

"How long was he-- Were you guys--?" I asked.

"It's okay. I know it's weird and isn't okay. That's why I needed to tell someone. I was placed there at eleven years old, before my twelfth birthday. He started as soon as my social worker placed me there. He didn't start with sex, but quickly moved us along."

"Did your foster mom know?" I asked.

"I don't know. Sometimes I thought yes, because she was always mean to me for a couple of days after. But then, all the sudden, it would be like nothing happened. My foster parents were strange. Wendy slept in one bedroom and Josh slept in another. Wendy was really, really, large. She walked very slow and with a walker. I don't think she could have moved fast enough to catch us in the act."

"Did you ever tell him you didn't like it?"

"At first, yes, but as the years passed, I started actually liking it. I liked the *us*. I liked how he treated me and made me feel special. Until . . . Until I learned I wasn't his first. First child . . . I was jealous, I was angry, I was confused, and I was sad. That's when I did it. I tried to shoot myself. I grabbed my foster dad's gun. With the barrel to my temple, I pulled the trigger and nothing happened. My foster mom, Wendy, freaked out and called 911. Josh left the house. I haven't seen them since."

"I'm so sorry! I'm glad Ray never tried anything like that with me. Someone in one of my foster homes wasn't so lucky though."

"What are you going to do? You have to tell someone. My Mama taught me something that helped when I needed to turn Ian in. She said, "Always do what's right, baby. It ain't right to hurt nobody.""

"I think about that all the time."

"I want to tell Dr. Lydia, but was hoping you would come with me to tell her. I don't want to do it alone."

"Of course, I will come with you."

And, that was pretty much my day. I was pickled after everything but promised I would help Olivia talk to Dr. Lydia tomorrow after some much needed shut-eye.

Not looking forward to it,

Eva

Dear Kami,

Olivia's situation is dire. Dr. Lydia was upset when she heard the news. She told Olivia and I it makes her sad to hear about adults who hurt the children they are entrusted to care for. Dr. Lydia's eyes got watery and I could see the sadness. I could see her trying to swallow and control it. I used to do that when Ray hit Mama and me, control the sadness.

Dr. Lydia asked me to return to my normal routine while she finished with Olivia. Dr. Lydia wanted to document all the details of Olivia's abuse before the social workers and police got too involved.

She asked me to think about how this made me feel about my own situation and past abuse.

I've never been raped. I can't imagine it.

Ray used to rape Mama. She wouldn't admit to it, but when someone is yelling and crying, begging you to stop, it's not called consensual. He hurt her so bad one time, she couldn't sit down without pain for a week.

And, when a grown man has his way with a child, I know *that* isn't consensual.

Mama always made excuses for him saying he's just an old drunk. I guess that was all she *could* say. What other excuse could you have to let someone abuse your kid while you stand by and watch or ignore it?

He never abused me the same way he did Mama although I felt raped at times. When he made me take my clothes off to finish my chores, so I wouldn't have any place to hide books, I felt dead, like I wanted to give up, defeated and empty. I don't know how I kept going. Maybe because I knew I had to for Mama.

I remember *the* day. I will never forget it, people scurrying around the property, collecting evidence and taking interviews. I remember Ray's scowl as he sat in the backseat of the police cruiser. I could see him through the kitchen window as I sat in shock. The social worker kept repeating the question, "Did you tell the three men your name is Idiot?"

I nodded because if I opened my mouth to say yes, I would cry.

I would never forget the numbness I felt when I saw the hunters and when they saw me. They saw all of me. Ray made me strip again that day and it was freezing outside. I had been trying to cut wood as fast as I could to stay warm, but it was too cold out. I was sitting at the base of a tree hugging my knees and breathing into them trying to keep warm.

I was bleeding between my legs and they assumed I had been raped with all the bruises, nicks, and cuts. I heard the man with the beard whisper to the man wearing the hoodie that he thought I'd been raped. They asked me where I lived, but I was shivering, so I pointed in the direction of the house. One of the hunters wrapped me in a blanket and carried me home.

Ray spotted us and came out crazed and yelling, arms flailing everywhere. The men knew the situation was bad. Ray tried to grab me from their arms, but they refused to let me go. They used a portable handheld radio to contact the police.

Once the police interviewed Mama, she broke down and told them about Ray calling me Idiot and about the other abuse. She said she tried stopping him for years, but never could.

That's when Ray went to jail, and Mama made her way to a rehab and parenting program.

This is when I went silent. That's what the social worker called it anyway. I was quiet until I ended up with Evelyn and Bob. I really liked them.

TTYL,

Eva

Dear Kami,

Thank God for a free weekend! Because we've all been working so hard, Dr. Lydia surprised us all with weekend passes.

Except for Olivia. She can't leave because of the situation. She has been talking to person-after-person about her foster dad. She seems okay though.

I am excited because Melissa is coming to take me out for lunch and a movie. She found a great soup and salad place she told me about. I love soup! I like salad too, but just the lettuce with vinegar on top. I like all kinds of vinegar. I promised Olivia I would bring her back something good to eat.

Melissa said there's a new movie out called, *A Dog's Purpose*. She said it looks good. I've never had a dog of my own, but one of the foster families I lived with had a Labradoodle. Maybe it was a Goldendoodle, IDK. One of the two. His name was Sparky. I really liked him, and I think he liked me. He always seemed to follow me around. I didn't mind though because I had no other friends in the house. The family was nice, but they didn't take kids permanently. They only accepted respite placements.

Dr. Lydia said she and Melissa wanted to meet with me before our outing. That made me a little nervous, but Dr. Lydia promised it wasn't anything to be nervous about.

I was excited about seeing Melissa! Only ten minutes until she would arrive. Wait! I know I smell vanilla! That's either someone's tasty snack or Melissa is early. She always wears this vanilla scented lotion from Bath & Body Works. I really like it!

It's her! I hear her voice! I'd recognize it anywhere!

"Oh, my God! It's you! Meet my friend Olivia."

"Olivia, this is Melissa. She's my guidance counselor."

"Hi Melissa. Eva talks about you all the time!"

I blushed.

I'm not sure why I blushed, but I did.

"Nice to meet you, Olivia! Eva, lets head to Dr. Lydia's office. There's something I'd like to discuss with you before we go to lunch."

"Okay. Am I in trouble?"

"In trouble for what? From what I'm hearing, you're doing great in here. Don't worry. It's good. Trust me."

I like Dr. Lydia, but her office always smells like feet and I figured out why. She has spare shoes in her office. Sometimes she wears high heels to important meetings. She always changes into flats before she makes her rounds though. Her flat shoes stink. She wears them without socks. Sometimes I think I should tell her, but then I assume she must know and doesn't care. I can tell Melissa smells it too. She's too nice to say anything though.

Once we got through all the greetings, she did it. Melissa had a way of making my head reel. She did a number on me this time, *that's* for sure!

"Eva, are you okay? What are you thinking?" asked Dr. Lydia.

I sat quietly for a few minutes and then whispered with a sob, "They want *me*? Why me? I have a *real* family?"

Melissa was trying her best to fight back a wall of tears. She wasn't wearing make-up, so I knew she planned this. She didn't want black streaks smudged down her face during lunch. What can I say? She's predictable.

"Melissa, why does a family want *me*? Do they know about all of my issues?"

"Of course, they know about you. They know the good and bad, but I figured I'd let you show them what a great person you really are. Do you remember Dr. Paxton?"

"Isn't she the school shrink?"

"Yes. She is the school psychologist. She and her husband want to adopt you."

"Adopt? Not foster? Why?"

"Eva, Dr. Paxton is one of my best friends. I've talked with her extensively about you. She and Ed, her husband, don't want you to ever worry about not having a place to call home. Dr. Paxton, Rose, mentioned adopting you before, but the time never seemed right. Until now."

"They have two biological children. One is a sophomore in college and the other just graduated. If you're okay with the adoption, Rose will retire. Ed will keep working because he's a work-a-holic." Melissa continued, "This would be the perfect place for you, Eva. I can't imagine a better outcome."

"Wh--When do they want to adopt me?"

"They would like to start the process now, while you're here. They wanted to know if you would like to stay overnight with them when you earn overnight weekend passes."

"Would I have to go there by myself? Could you come with me?"

"I can take you there and stay for a while, but I want you to really get to know them. They are super people. They want to get to know you too."

"They aren't scared of me with all of my problems?"

"No, Eva. They are excited about the possibility of welcoming you into their family."

"What if I don't like them?"

"Adoption will never be forced, Eva, but I don't think that will be an issue. If I did, I wouldn't have even considered the option."

Just then, Dr. Lydia interjected, "Melissa and I believe this is a great opportunity for you. You certainly deserve it! We wanted to bring this up before your outing to give you time to process everything and talk it over. I need to move on to my next meeting. I've been very busy since Olivia's news. You *do* realize she decided to do the right thing and tell because of you, right? Your bravery inspired her to do the same. To be brave. I better go now. I don't want to be late. You two have fun. And, yes, it's fine for you to bring food back for Olivia but please limit the caffeine."

"Okay, thanks Dr. Lydia! We should get going too if we want to eat before the movie."

Feeling overwhelmed,

Eva

Dear Kami,

After the movie . . . After the movie . . . After the movie . . .

I cried my eyes out. I cried so much, Melissa stopped by a convenience store to buy me a box of Kleenex. I used half the box. I don't think I've ever cried that much in my life.

Melissa cried, but not as much as me.

Once I calmed down, Melissa told me crying is good. She said I probably needed to have a really good cry with all of the major things happening in my life. Not bad things, just big things.

Melissa said I've been through more in my short sixteen, almost seventeen years than most people go through in a lifetime.

Before we headed back to the hospital, we stopped to pick up Olivia's food. She was craving a burger and fries, so we drove through a fast food place and ordered a large fry and a double burger with no Mayo.

Once I was checked back into the hospital, I said goodbye to Melissa and headed to Olivia's room, so I could give her food and tell her my news. I didn't expect the reaction I got from her when I told her about the possible adoption. She called me stupid and said it would never work. She said I'm just setting myself up to get my heart broken.

It's almost like she was mad at me.

Evelyn and Bob used to call things they couldn't explain or things that made no sense *the twilight zone*. That's exactly how I felt about Olivia's rant. It's twilight zone shit for sure. Oh well! At least she said thanks for the burger and fries.

Why are people so confusing? I miss you, Kami. I miss our fun times and uncomplicated friendship.

I like Olivia. I hope she doesn't stay mad.

For the first time in a while, I wanted to curl up under my bed with a blanket. I just needed a break! I needed quiet. There were always people around. When you have people, you have people noises. Never any quiet. Not real quiet.

Thankfully, I was in a room with a regular bed and not just a mattress on a concrete slab. I hated those rooms.

I was considered one of the trusted patients, so I guess the white coats weren't afraid I'd try to off myself any time soon.

I stashed my blanket and pillow under the bed just in time for one of the white coats to walk by and ask me what I was doing. Never any quiet!

Time to stop writing and enjoy the much-needed quiet time under my bed. I hope I am lucky enough to catch some ZZZ's.

Crying is such hard work! Dealing with people is harder though.

Under the bed I go,

Eva

Dear Kami,

The twilight zone is such a strange place! It's a place of unintended consequences, unexplained expectations, unsaid anger, and people noise. It's hard to believe someone can be so assertive and certain in one circumstance, and a one hundred percent total nut in another. Olivia's craze shocked me, although I'm not sure why. She *is* here after all.

I've seen enough crazy shit in my life, nothing should shock me. But, that's not how life works. I still get shocked, surprised, hurt, and angered despite the fact I know humans aren't perfect and I expect them to let me down.

Harry and Billy had been avoiding all situations involving Olivia and I being in the same vicinity for more than a routine or prescribed amount of time. Harry told me he thinks Olivia is Jealous because I am going to have an adoptive family. He said she had been saying she wished her baby had grandparents.

I didn't say anything to Harry about the father of Olivia's baby because I didn't think it was my place. Olivia's situation is not their business, and not my business to tell. That would be a lot like one of the foster kids reading my diary and telling people what they read. I had that happen and it didn't feel good. It was one of the most horrific experiences in my life.

If Olivia stays mad, or jealous, or whatever is going on to make her avoid me, I don't want to stay here. It blows without her. We just formed a group of friends, and until now, everything has been so much easier without Molly.

Although I've been spending alone time under my bed, Harry and Billy made it a point to stop by for our newly established evening rants. We mostly talk about the white coats, Dr. Lydia, and Olivia. Although she speaks to Billy and Harry, they spend a lot of time with me, so that limits the time she would normally spend with them.

I asked Billy and Harry if I should try to talk to Olivia, but they said it would be better to let her come to me when she's ready. That makes it sound like she's still pretty mad, sad, jealous, or whatever. Let her come to me when she's ready! I have enough of my own shit to deal with, I certainly don't need this too.

I like talking to Olivia. I could use her friendship right now, but at least I have Harry and Billy. They're good to talk to, but it's not the same. I thought she and I had something special. Why is life so confusing? And hard?

Shouldn't living be easier? Should everything be such a struggle? Sometimes even breathing is hard to do.

I wish I could talk to Melissa right now. I know I can't though. I have to cooperate with everyone if I want to continue to visit her. Maybe Dr. Lydia will have time to talk?

That's what I was wondering, as I headed down the noisy hallway toward her office. That's when I saw *her* sitting there. Olivia was also waiting to see Dr. Lydia. I rolled my eyes as I whipped around and started to turn the corner, but not before she spotted me.

"Hi, Stranger! You don't have to hide just because I think you're being stupid ya know."

"Um, well, I'm not. Not really."

"I don't know what you call it then, but where I come from, when someone goes out of their way to make sure they don't see you, it's called hiding."

"C'mere. I have news."

"You-- You want to talk to me now?"

"Of course! Don't mind my pregnancy hormones. You know I love ya!" Olivia chuckled.

"What's your news?"

"The police took my foster father into custody for questioning. Dr. Lydia said the judge isn't likely to make me face him directly. She said I can either deliver my testimony via video or in his or her chambers."

"That's good," I replied.

"I'm really sorry for calling you stupid. I know that kind of name calling hits a sensitive spot for you. I am sorry."

GTG,

Eva

Dear Kami,

Things are finally starting to settle down around here after the bombshell Olivia dropped.

I am still the only person besides Dr. Lydia she has talked to about it though. As I said before, it's not my news to share, so the others won't hear it from me.

I'm pretty excited and nervous about this weekend. I have my first weekend visit with the Paxton's. Melissa is taking me to their house on Friday.

News of the possible adoption makes me think of Mama a lot. Melissa said the social workers searched for her recently, but as usual, had no luck. There are so many things I want to ask her. I mostly want to tell her how much I love her though. I will always love her. What I would give to hear her call me her little Princess again!

Melissa said the Paxton's two daughters are supposed to show up for dinner and to meet me. I hope they're nice! One is in college and the other just graduated. I hope they like me. They're older than me anyway, so it's not like they'll wanna hang out or anything.

Before I leave for the weekend, I have to sign a contract. Everyone's contracts are different when they start earning over-night visits. Mine basically says I will avoid weed and agree to drug test when I return. It also says if I start feeling depressed, I will call Melissa or Dr. Lydia. It's kind of a funny goal, but Dr. Lydia wants me to try at least one new food while I am there.

Melissa said I can end the visit at any time if I am not comfortable.

For now, I am just glad Olivia isn't jealous about my weekend visit. I know her hormones are working overtime though because she has been on a roll with Frankie. Every time Frankie even tries to whine about something, Olivia goes all Tasmania on her. I think she scares Frankie, which I like. Harry is excited for me. He thinks this is the best thing that could ever happen to me. Billy seems less excited, but I think that's just his blahhh personality.

I am surprised I have so many friends in here. People actually like me for me. And, I like them back. I *like* liking them back most of the time. The only time I really don't is when there is drama. People create drama. Drama creates bad feelings and panic attacks. Ughhh, something Billy and I understand well.

I hope the Paxton's like me. I hope I like them.

Anxious,

Eva

Dear Kami,

It's about midnight on Friday, and I am under the bed at the Paxton's. I don't really know what to think about everything. I mean, it is great. Wonderful . . . There's just so much to process.

Like, the fact that I am sleeping in what may be my future bedroom, under my future bed. I think I am overwhelmed. I have been laying here for at least thirty minutes and I can't sleep.

I know she asked me to call her Rose, but I still think of her as Dr. Paxton. Ed was funny and made everyone laugh a lot. I met the Paxton's daughters, Halee and Ki. Halee is still in college but Ki recently graduated. Ki is looking into graduate programs where she wants to study some kind of design.

Halee has this wild hair with soft brown tight spirals ringing down her back. She is gorgeous! Ki's hair is a deep chocolate color that matches her eyes. Her curls are loose, flowing, and are absolutely delightful. They smell like apples!

Arrghh! I need sleep. Bad. My mind is working overtime. I am going to stop writing and try to force myself to rest.

This house is so nice! This family is so nice! This feels like a dream!

C'mon dreamland,

Eva

Dear Kami,

Ki and Halee left today after breakfast. They seem like a lot of fun. They live together in the next town over where they rent a house. They invited me to stay the night with them sometime. They mentioned pizza and movies.

They think I am strange because I don't like pizza. I promised them I would try it again. I have only had pizza twice. The first time I tried it was at a restaurant where they piled meat and anchovies on top. It was disgusting! The second time was with Evelyn and Bob. It was a frozen pizza and had a funny smell. I took a bite, but spit it out. Ki said their neighborhood pizza place is to die for. I don't know about *that*, but I will at least try it.

Before they left, Halee told me she is excited about having another sister. That made me happy!

Rose and Ed took me out for dinner. We went to their favorite restaurant, which is now my favorite restaurant. They said they knew I would like it because it is a buffet that has salad, soup, plain cheese pizza, meat, all kinds of veggies, and dessert. I ate so much! I'd go get one or two things, scarf it down, and go back for more. I caught Rose watching me eat and smiling.

I think they really like me. I really like them! I hope this adoption works out. I couldn't get any luckier!

They want to take me shopping next time I visit. I hate shopping for clothes because I don't like the way I look in most of them. I'll probably hate clothes shopping, but I get to pick bedroom furniture and decorations. I said the furniture looked fine to me, but Rose said, "I want you to have your very own room and want you to love it. You can pick out anything you want."

I have never thought about bedroom furniture or decorations. Rose wants me to start thinking about paint colors. How am I supposed to know what looks good and what doesn't? Olivia! She'll help me! That is, if her hormones aren't holding her brain hostage.

This weekend is flying by! I can't believe it's coming to an end and I have to go back so soon.

Billy, Olivia, and Harry will like hearing about my weekend. I just hope Olivia doesn't freak out on me again!

Rose said Melissa will be here tomorrow morning to pick me up and take me back. Before I headed to my room for the night, Rose hugged me. It was awkward at first, but then, I let it happen. I hugged her back and I liked it. It felt like home.

Happy,

Eva

Dear Kami,

I am so confused! Can humans possibly get any more fucked up? Hormones, opinions, jealousy, fear . . . Damn . . .Aren't we a mess! There are good ones out there like Melissa, Evelyn and Bob, and the Paxton's, but I believe they're few and far between.

Time for Sunday afternoon quiet time! The white coats are strict about quiet time. We can use the time to catch up on assignments, sleep, write in our journals, read, or draw. The rules are that we must do whatever we're doing alone, we must be silent, and we must be in our assigned rooms.

I'm beat! Under the bed I go for a much-needed nap!

Aaawaawh! Stretch, yawn again, and re-position. I'll ponder life's crazies when I wake!

That was a *hell* of a nap! I feel like puking purple. A lot of purple. Purple everywhere, kind-of-purple. And, with that puki-purple feeling, in she blows like the infamous devil-wind.

"You've been sleeping? All I've been able to do is think about designing a room for my baby. Sorry I snapped when you said that looks like too much purple! I mean, you can *never* have too much purple!"

"That's okay. I had a dream about having a purple bedroom though. And, it made me feel nauseous," I laughed.

I was secretly glad my laughing didn't make her mad.

Just as the thought escaped my mind, Harry walked in and asked, "So, what color *are* you thinking of for the babies' room?"

Olivia squealed, rushed over to Harry, hugged him and said, "Rainbow colored of course. Help us look on Pinterest after dinner! This is so exciting, don't you think?"

Harry smiled, quickly glanced my way, winked, and exaggeratedly said, "Of course it's fun and exciting!"

Olivia laughed, snapped her fingers, and slipped out of her house shoes so she was wearing only fuzzy socks. She said, "Watch this guys," as she slid all the way down the newly waxed hallway floors, almost making it to her room until one of the white coats grabbed her.

"Hon, you *know* that is dangerous. You must be more careful. You're thinking for two now."

Olivia ducked her head and replied, "Yes ma'am."

Harry hung back in my room and asked, "So, you're not too keen on all of the purple, huh?"

"No, and I didn't see anything else I liked either," I semi-whined, disgusting myself further.

"C'mon! I'll help you look. We have about fifteen minutes until dinner. We'll hit up Pinterest again."

"You're good at this, ya know? How did you *know* I would like it?" I asked in jaw- dropping amazement.

"Well, you spent about ten minutes showing me everything you didn't like, so I was able to figure out what colors, fabrics, and patterns to avoid. I think you're a classic minimalist."

"A what?" I asked.

"A minimalist is someone who doesn't like a lot of stuff. You know, clutter."

"I like clean and simple. Too much stuff everywhere makes me nervous."

"So, you're basically a white down comforter, two pillows, and white wall person," Harry interjected.

"Yeah, I'd eventually like to put some of my art work on the walls, but not too much, ya know… It's the clutter thing again," I laughed.

"Let's go get dinner! Whatcha wanna bet Olivia will think my room décor is stupid?" I said.

"Ah! She may. She's opinionated like that. She apologizes when she's out of line at least.

Anyway, who cares! It's going to be *your* room, not hers."

Dinner here we come,

Eva

Dear Kami,

The first thing Dr. Lydia asked me about when I saw here earlier was the goal of trying at least one new food. I told her about the buffet and about the single chick-pea I put on my tongue and promptly spit back out. I can't remember ever trying such a bland and dry pea, bean, or whatever it was.

Dr. Lydia laughed and said she can't stand them either. She added, "I think they're so terrible, someone changed the name from garbanzo beans to chick peas hoping they would catch on. The big fad now is trying to convince children to eat them in the name of health. I'll stick to black beans, pintos, and kidney beans. I'll never be a fan of chick peas and I don't blame you for not liking them. Good job trying something new though."

I told her about Ki and Halee inviting me over to their house for pizza. She couldn't believe I've only tried it twice and didn't like it either time. I also told her about the Paxton's wanting to take me shopping for clothes and bedroom furniture and about how Harry helped me find a style I liked.

She said, "Eva, you've come so far since you've been here. With these life changes facing you, I want you to take the rest of the week and focus solely on you. I want you focusing on feelings, not on paint colors, okay . . . Don't get me wrong, paint colors are fun, but I don't want that taking away from the important work you should be doing that focuses on how you feel, why you feel, what you feel, and when you feel. This is super important work. If you start feeling overwhelmed, come find me and we'll talk about it. I really want you thinking about your Mom, Ray, your Mom's apparent drug use and homelessness, and Ray's abuse."

"You're also going to need to think about the situation with Ian and delve into how you feel about not seeing him, about him being your first sexual partner, and the school shooting scenario. I want you to think about how you've changed since then and how you feel about the changes. This may be difficult, but think about how your Mom could have done things differently to protect you from Ray. Think about what you want to learn from the Paxton's and how you want to continue to grow. Focus on where you want to be in thirty days, sixty days, ninety days, a year, and five years. Think about your Mom and how she would feel about the adoption."

"Finally, think of three things you have accomplished since you have been here and are proud of. I know it's a tall order, but you're not going to be here forever, Eva. I need to know you're ready and equipped to handle what you'll be faced with out there."

So, FML! I guess I still need to go to group counseling, but instead of any homework regularly assigned, I am to focus on the things Dr. Lydia mentioned. She wants to review my journals and meet with me before I spend another weekend away."

I'm glad I get weekend passes. We just got two new people on our floor, and they're both annoying. One girl cries all of the time and the other literally just smeared shit all over her walls and floor. I guess she pooped, reached in with her bare hands and started drawing poop stick figure people.

It takes all kinds, I suppose!

It reeks on our floor now. I think the smell of her shit is permanently burned in my nose.

The Paxton's house smells so nice. It's the nicest and largest house I've ever been in. I can't believe I am going to be living there! I have to admit, I'm pretty excited about having my own room too!

Oops! I hear the alarm. The cra-cra, newbie, shit-smearer must be up to something else. If she creates another stinky mess, I'm not going to be happy. Plus, I am tired of seeing Billy walk around with a wooden safety clothes pin on his nose.

Sigh . . .

Got a lot to think about,

Eva

Dear Kami,

Dr. Lydia gave me a lot to think about. How am I supposed to know why I feel what I feel? The only thing I know for sure right now is that I feel overwhelmed with all of this stuff I am supposed to write about. I know why I feel overwhelmed, but that's about it.

This is one of those days I wish we could be magically transported back to the creek bank. We could draw and read.

I don't know how I really feel about not seeing Ian. I mean, he *is* in jail. It's not like I'd be able to see him a lot anyway. And, he really wanted to hurt people. Kill people. I'm not okay with that. That is something I will *never* be okay with. I am glad he is getting the help he needs. God knows he needs it. We both need it. I am fucked up too, but Dr. Lydia thinks I am making progress.

I need to think about hot chocolate and a fire for a while. This is too much to deal with. Plus, I'm getting a headache.

I will try to focus on this stuff again later,

Eva

Dear Kami,

I'm feeling a little better now. I was able to calm down and relax. I don't really know what I feel about Mama's drug use and homelessness. She never used drugs when I was little. At least, I don't think she did. I wish she would get clean and find a place to live. I worry about her and I will always love her; she's my mom. Sometimes I wonder if I will ever see her again. It has been so long since I've seen her.

If she got into meth, she may look a lot different by now. Meth is scary. People who use it look terrible. And scary. It makes their teeth fall out, they end up with huge craters in their face, and the shape of their face changes from losing their teeth. I don't know why anyone would do meth. Plus, I think it's made from drain cleaner and other nasty chemicals.

As far as how she would feel about me getting adopted . . . She would be happy. She always wanted the best for me. She would like the Paxton's. She would have loved Evelyn and

Bob too. She'd be thankful for them teaching me so much and really focusing on my education. Mama taught me to read and write. She would be proud of me. I read and write much better than she used to. I'm glad she gave me such a wonderful gift.

Dr. Lydia wants me to think about how Mama could have protected me from Ray. She did! She always tried. I used to beg her to move away, but I think she always secretly hoped he would change. I wish she would have just quit her job, so I wasn't left behind with Ray while she worked. We could have left so many times when he was in his drunken stupors. If we would have, it would be Mama and me now. There would have been no Ian, no school shooting plot, and no nut-ward. I'd be okay with that!

I'll write more later. Harry just came in and is super upset. He just found out his parents are sending him to a therapeutic boarding school all the way across the country when he gets out of here. I've never seen him so upset.

TTYL,

Eva

Dear Kami,

I don't know if I can help Harry. He wants to run away so he doesn't have to go to that boarding school.

Oh, here he comes again. I can see him walking up the hallway. I'm sure he's heading to my room.

"Hi," I said, hoping to gauge his mood by his response. "How are you doing?" I asked.

"Well, besides the fact that my parents want to send me off across the country to a school I've never seen, I guess as good as I can be. I always knew they hated being around me. It's like I creep them out or something and they want to send me away, so they don't have to deal with me. Oh shit! Do I hear Olivia? Can we go somewhere else, so she doesn't see us? I can't deal with her pregnancy drama right now."

"Yeah, come on. We'll go to the lending library. I've never seen her in there," I replied.

"Okay. Thanks. I love Olivia to death, but I'm not in the mood right now!"

"I understand. I really do."

"I know Eva. I feel bad for even complaining to you because you've been through so much. I can't imagine going through even a

101

fraction of what you have. My parents are such assholes. They'd rather spend 10k a month to send me off, so I don't embarrass them, than to love me as I am."

"This isn't a who's been through worse competition. I don't know what I would do if I had a parent who didn't want me. That was never the case with me. My Mama loved me."

"You always make me feel better, Eva. Thank you for being my friend."

"Yeah, you too," I laughed. "I've never been good at making friends. Most people are too high maintenance."

"I know. I really hate asking, but I am going to need you to help me get out of here. I'm not staying around and waiting for my parents to send me off."

"Wha--What do you want me to do?"

"I've been thinking, and I believe my only way out is to steal the roving night nurse's car. I can distract her during pill call and you can grab the keys off the board in the nurse's station."

"Oh, holy shit! I'm not doing that!"

"Please, I have to get out of here soon."

"No. I--I can't. I won't! Where will you go?"

"My cousin ran away to New Jersey years ago. She's eighteen or nineteen now. She wrote me a letter about six months ago. I lifted it from the mailbox before my parents found it and I memorized her address. If I can make it there, she has a friend named Marty Block who may help me. He helped her. He even bought her a bus ticket to get there."

"Maybe I can distract the nurse by asking for a Tylenol or something. I am not going to do anything that will get me caught though."

"That would be good. I just have to get out of here soon. Dr. Lydia said my parents hired someone to transport me to the boarding school. They're not even planning to see me before I go! She said the transporter would use handcuffs to ensure I don't try to run away. So, see, I have to leave this place. I like it here, but I have to leave."

"When are you planning to do this?"

"In about an hour and a half. I have to do it tonight."

"Oh my God! Wow. I wasn't expecting you to want to leave today."

"Please, Eva."

"Okay. When the evening nurse arrives, before she doles out meds, I'll go ask her for

Tylenol. I'll need one by then after all of this. That's all I am doing though."

"Thank you! I am going to shower and put on a few layers of clothes, so I won't get cold."

"Wait, Harry. Don't you think the police will catch you?"

"Not if I ditch the car as soon as I can and hitch a ride with someone."

"Do you even know how to drive a car?"

"Of course. My grandpa taught me to drive."

"Won't you miss him?"

"He's dead."

FML,

Eva

Dear Kami,

What have I gotten myself into? Apparently, Harry made it out because we're all locked in our rooms while they search for him.

After I asked for the Tylenol, Olivia stopped by. The white coats noticed Harry missing about twenty minutes after that. I'm the only one who knows what's really going on, and it's an eerie feeling. Olivia thinks we're being locked in our rooms because of something one of the new girls did. I didn't say I knew any different.

Damn Harry. I guess I understand though. It would suck being sent away when you have a family!

I wonder how long they will keep us locked in? I guess it doesn't matter because it will be time for lights-out soon anyway.

If this isn't an under my bed moment, I don't know what is. I know the white coats want us *on* our beds, so they can see us when they do the nightly count, but I don't care. I'm getting under my bed with my pillow and blanket now.

I'll write more later,

Eva

Dear Kami,

FML! Dr. Lydia just left my room. She asked me if I had any idea where Harry was. She asked Billy and Olivia first, I guess. I heard her closing the door to their rooms before she came into mine. Of course, neither of them know anything.

I told her everything. Well, maybe not *everything*. I told her everything excluding the part about me asking for Tylenol and distracting the nurse.

Harry promised he would never rat me out if he were to get caught. He doesn't want my chances of being adopted to be compromised. He knows I am planning to tell his whereabouts if asked. I wouldn't *volunteer* the info, but I wouldn't lie either.

He has likely already ditched the car somewhere anyway.

Dr. Lydia contacted Harry's parents and the police to put out an APB. I couldn't tell if Dr. Lydia was mad or just scared for Harry. Maybe she's just tired.

Although I'm sure she realizes it's not going to happen, she told me to try to get some sleep. Right! Back under the bed I go.

Later,

Eva

Dear Kami,

Morning rang in with white coats scurrying around everywhere. Everyone was buzzing around during breakfast with curious anxiety. Groups of people were huddled together at tables whispering back and forth.

Of course, Olivia had to interject her two cents. "I heard Harry ran away with a nurse," she quipped.

"I have no idea what happened. I hope he is okay," I replied.

My generic response earned me a confused and blank look. Thankfully, she didn't follow it up with further questioning. She's like a police interrogator sometimes.

Dr. Lydia walked into the cafeteria and announced, "As you're all aware, we have a bit of a situation on our hands. We will brief everyone in fifteen minutes in your respective groups. Please gather accordingly."

I was sweating bullets hoping Dr. Lydia wouldn't spill the beans about me knowing Harry's plan. She didn't. Whew! She gave us information that sent chills up and down my spine though. She said Harry's parents informed her Harry's cousin ran away years before with the help of her thirty-something-year-old pimp. Harry's cousin met him online and he lured her into prostitution.

My heart was pounding.

Group was over, and I had to talk to Dr. Lydia. I had to know if she had the pimp's name.

She asked why I wanted to know, and I said, "Harry said he was hoping someone named Marty Block would help him."

"That's it!" exclaimed Dr. Lydia. "That's the name Harry's parents mentioned. He is Harry's cousin's pimp. The one who lured her into prostitution and drugs. I have to let his parents know. Thank you for coming forward, Eva. I know you are going through a lot right now. I need to call them. This is extremely serious."

I felt cold sweat beading up on my upper lip and forehead.

I felt a panic attack coming on and I could not force myself to think about hot chocolate or a campfire for the life of me!

What have I gotten myself into,

Eva

* * *

Dear Kami,

That panic attack came on like lightning, strong and fast. Billy always seems to be in the right place at the right time. He sure came around for me this time and didn't leave my side. He's so good at knowing what to do and how to help. He helped me get my breathing back under control and gently massaged my scalp as he spoke. His words and gentle touch eased my anxiety long enough to make me feel better, but the touching soon became more than I could handle.

I pictured him picking his nose, eating a booger, and then rubbing my head. I had to shower and wash my hair! I couldn't stand the thought of booger-goop in my hair. Maybe that isn't the nicest thought, but I've seen him pick and eat boogers, so it's not too far off.

Olivia keeps wanting to gossip about Harry. I have to be careful not to accidentally hint I know anything about the situation. I'd never hear the end of it if she knew. She has gotten so motherly since her pregnancy. I can't imagine ever being pregnant. Thank God, I dodged *that* bullet!

Now, I get the treat of sitting through art therapy with Olivia wanting to gossip and being over-motherly.

FML!

I usually like art therapy, but I just couldn't get into it today. My head is with Harry. I hope he is okay.

Oh! The white coats are ringing the bell to let us know we need to gather in the day room. I wonder if they found Harry?

TTYL,

Eva

Dear Kami,

They found him! They said the police intercepted him on a greyhound bus a few states away. They are keeping him at a local juvenile detention center until his parents make arrangements for him. He can't come back here because he ran from here. That's one of the rules. If you run, you don't get a second chance. I hope he will be okay. Wherever he ends up will be better than life as a prostitute would be. I wonder if he knew his cousin was into prostitution and had a pimp? Who knows . . . I don't know him well enough to assume.

And, Olivia was in full gossip mode. The story evolved from running away with a nurse to running away to work for a pimp, maybe even *be* a pimp. I wonder if I will ever see him again? He was the best friend I had in this place. Billy and Olivia are both fine, I just had a special connection with Harry.

With all the commotion, Dr. Lydia stopped by my room and asked me to be in her office in fifteen minutes. I silently gasp and wonder what she wants now.

Curiosity was obviously getting the best of Olivia because she offered, "I'll go with you if you'd like."

I sighed, "It's okay, it's probably nothing anyway."

"Well, if you need me, you know where to find me," she insisted.

I said thanks and headed over to Dr. Lydia's office. The door was closed, and I was early. I didn't care though because it got me away from Mother Olivia.

When Dr. Lydia finally opened the door, Melissa was sitting there. I was shocked! I didn't expect to see Melissa until my next home visit with the Paxton's.

Dr. Lydia could see I was starting to get nervous, so she quickly interjected, "Melissa is here to spend some time with you and to help process everything that has happened over the last couple of days. You're doing so well, we want to make sure you don't slip backwards with Harry leaving so abruptly."

I hugged Melissa and I think it shocked her! She hugged me back, of course. I'm not usually the overly huggy type, but I needed it then. And it was nice.

Dr. Lydia stayed for about five minutes and then left us while she made her rounds.

"How are you holding up? Dr. Lydia says you're doing well," said Melissa.

"I'm okay. Just a lot to think about. Paint colors, shopping, how, why, when, and what I feel about *everything*. Now Harry."

"I know the Paxton's are excited about taking you shopping, but if it's causing too much stress right now, it's something that can be done later. It's not an urgent matter. I didn't realize you were so close to Harry."

"We've gotten closer these last couple of months," I replied.

"I am proud of you for telling Dr. Lydia what you knew about Harry leaving. You likely saved his life."

"Yeah, they say I am good at that. And at being a snitch," I quickly spouted.

"You're not a snitch, Eva. You're someone with a whole hell of a lot of life experience that frankly, sucks. You've made the most out of those experiences by saving lives. You saved countless, innocent lives from being senselessly slain at the high school, and if Harry would have gotten thrown into prostitution, he would have very little chance of making it out alive. You are a good person, Eva. A very good person. I am proud to know you."

"You're proud to know someone who lost their virginity to a guy who planned to shoot up a school?" I said sarcastically.

"I am proud to know someone who saved lives and who inspired another resident to do the right thing also. Olivia likely only told-on her foster father because of the brave acts she knew you accomplished. And, who cares who you lost your virginity to? I certainly don't," she replied.

"Are you still going to be proud to know me when I tell you that although I lost my virginity to Ian, I think I am a lesbian? I *hated* sex with Ian. The thought of a dick makes me sick. And, they are ugly. Yep, I'm a lesbian! I'm a lesbian at heart, but have never been with a girl. I like girls though. Girls like me. Not girls like Frankie, or the new girls… When I first met Olivia, I thought she was pretty and was attracted to her until she opened her mouth," I said almost like I was afraid I wouldn't say it if I didn't blurt it out.

It wasn't the reaction I expected but Melissa laughed and said, "You're not the first or only person in the world to be attracted to someone of the same sex. I've never talked to you about my sister, Layla, have I? Well, I'm about to! She was married three times before she realized the problem. They were all men! About a year after her last divorce, she met a wonderful woman named Amy. They have been together ever since and are happy as clams. True love is blinding. Anyway, my sis and Amy adopted a child together a few years ago. They named her Chloe. Without Layla and Amy, I wouldn't have my little Chloe. I'll love them forever for giving me a precious niece. I hope you find your own Amy one day. You deserve happiness."

So . . .

I cried. And cried . . .

I've never said I'm a lesbian out loud before. How weird. I somehow felt liberated. I think I've always been a lesbian, I just didn't realize it before. I didn't understand why I was always attracted to girls and never to dudes.

Melissa sat with me and handed me a box of Kleenex, "Here, you need these. It seems like I make you cry often anymore."

I laughed. And laughed . . .

The worst thing about crying was getting all snotty. I think I went through half the box before I could blow, and nothing would come out.

Melissa piped up, "Okay, before I go, name three things you've accomplished since you've been here. This will be one thing you can cross off your to-do list. I'll name the first thing. You admitted to yourself that you are a lesbian. That is a huge accomplishment in and of itself. It takes some people a lifetime and they still can't be honest with themselves."

"I guess the second thing is that I am making friends. I can't really think of anything else," I said.

"If you can't, I can. But, I'd like you to try. Don't make me be the one to tell you how awesome you are."

"Okay, I am learning how to deal with my panic attacks," I professed.

"That's a good one! There are so many things you've accomplished that come to mind. But, Dr. Lydia only asked for three, so for the sake of not overwhelming you more, let's just stick with those for now."

And, that was it. She left with the promise of picking me up on Friday for my weekend visit with Ed and Rose.

Later,

Eva

Dear Kami,

The visit I had with Melissa helped me a lot; they always do. She always knows exactly what and what *not* to say.

I know where I want to be in thirty days; that's easy. I'd like to accomplish my therapy goals and be closer to being ready for adoption. Since I'm not exactly sure when they will release me to live with the Paxton's, I'm not sure what my sixty to ninety-day goals should be.

Melissa said she thinks I'll be released from here before the adoption is final. She said the Paxton's don't want to wait until it's finalized, so they've agreed to foster me until that time.

Melissa said the adoption should be cut and dry because Mama's parental rights were terminated long ago.

In one year, I want to have most of my high school classes finished and want to make up classes I've missed. I'd like to go to college one day. Melissa said because I've been in foster care, I can go to college for free. She said it doesn't matter that I am being adopted, I can still go for free. That's good because I don't know how I would ever pay for it!

Things are starting to settle down a little around here. Harry's name isn't flying out of people's mouths every second word. Thank God!

Five years . . . How am I supposed to know what I want to be doing in five years? I'm not even seventeen yet! I guess I'd like to be in college or done with it.

Uggg! Dr. Lydia just told me Harry's parents asked if they could ask me questions about his plans. Thank God she told them that would never happen under any circumstance. She told them I'd already given all the information I had. I'd never help Harry's parents anyway. Not with the way they've treated him. They refuse to refer to him as Harry and still call him Heather. He hates it! Harry told me they are ashamed of him.

I thought he was strange at first only because I'd never met anyone like him. But, when you get to know him, you realize how much more he *is* like a he, minus having a dick, of course.

Off to group! I'll write later. I have to pack for my weekend visit with Rose and Ed, so I am not sure how much free time I'll have.

TTYL,

Eva

Dear Kami,

Melissa will be here at 4 p.m. to pick me up. I'll write either tonight or tomorrow!

Later,

Eva

Dear Kami,

Holy shit! I'm going shopping tomorrow! Ed and Rose are taking me shopping! I'm nervous, and then, my thoughts trail off and I think fondly of Harry. I am so happy he helped me find a style. A minimalist . . . I'm a minimalist.

Shopping for my bedroom should be easy, thanks to Harry. Clothes . . . That's another story.

I talked to Rose about the to-do list Dr. Lydia assigned. I told her I wasn't sure exactly what I wanted to learn from she and Ed. She helped me focus on a few things like learning to be loved and to love a forever family, learning to trust, and learning to feel safe inside the family unit. Wow! That's a tall order!

I am excited about going shopping. Excited and nervous!

And, I find myself under the bed again. I like this bed. I'd like to keep it if Ed and Rose say it's okay. It's the perfect height for making a nest under. Not too tall and not too short, but just right.

Rose knows I like to sleep under my bed sometimes and she's fine with it. She suggested we buy extra blankets and pillows to keep under there. I think I'm going to like it here!

I'm fading fast, so I'll write more tomorrow, and I'll tell you all about shopping.

Love,

Eva

Dear Kami,

OMG! I have *the most* comfortable comforter in the entire world! I wish you could see it. You would love it! Rose said it's the best down comforter Macy's sells. It's just like hers and Ed's. And my new sheets… I can't wait to feel how soft they will be once they're washed and dried. They are white with grey flowers.

I love my new fluffy rug so much. Rose suggested we also put one under my bed, so my nest is super comfy.

They said I can keep the furniture that's already in the room since I like it so much. It was Ki's furniture when she lived at home, but she said she didn't need it. Yay! So exciting!

I really have my *own* room. *My* room. I've never had a room of my own. My room with Mama and Ray was also a storage room.

Rose said I can do anything I want with my room, but I like it the way it is.

I have new clothes! I had a hard time finding anything that fit just rite at Macy's. And, mostly, I just didn't like the clothes. Rose said Ki and Halee love Old Navy and suggested we go there. I agreed because I'd never been. I loved it! They have all sizes and shapes of jeans. What does that mean? I found jeans that *actually* fit me. Yes, I did! I also found tee shirts and other shirts I love. Their shirts are so nice. And, their pajamas.

Rose and Ed helped me carry the bags, I bought so much stuff. I have never had so many new clothes. Mama used to pick things up from the thrift store for me from time to time. I always hated getting new things because they never fit right. I really like Old Navy. I see why Ki and Halee like it.

Rose said I can take anything I want back to the hospital with me when I go. I don't think I want to though. I don't want to get my hopes up and have it not work out. What if something happens and Rose and Ed change their minds, or the judge doesn't approve the adoption?

Before bed, Rose asked, "Why don't you want to take anything with you? It's all yours."

And, I told her, "What if something happens and you can't adopt me?"

She started crying, "Eva, there is nothing either of us want more. We already feel so much love for you, Sweetie. I know that may be difficult for you to understand. I don't know what I would do if we weren't allowed to adopt you. You are already such an important part of our family. Please don't ever think like that. I know it's hard. You've been through so much, my sweet girl. We would move the moon to make sure you're happy and safe. It will take time, but we will show you how much you belong with us."

With tears in my eyes, I replied, "Maybe I will take jeans and a few shirts."

Rose smiled and tucked me in for the night. I felt so comfortable and safe. She called me her sweet girl! I slept in *my* bed and had the best sleep I'd ever had in my young life. Wow!

We're going to meet Ki and Halee for breakfast.

TTYL,

Eva

Dear Kami,

Breakfast with Rose, Ed, Ki, and Halee was a culinary treat. We went to a place that had the best French toast I've ever had. Of course, I didn't want powdered sugar or syrup, and I asked for my strawberries on the side. The French toast created an explosion of the senses. I ate so much my stomach ached.

Ki and Halee are excited about seeing my new clothes and bedding, and I can't wait to show them.

After breakfast, Rose and Ed will drop me off at Melissa's house so she can take me back, so I'll have to show them my stuff next weekend. Halee said she was busy studying for final exams anyway, so it works out perfectly.

They both loved the outfit I was wearing. Ki liked it so much, she said she wanted to go buy something similar for herself.

We talked about my weekend, about Halee's classes, Ki's job, and about Rose retiring. That's when Rose told me about her idea to retire and homeschool me. She asked what I thought about it. "Would you be okay with not attending a traditional public high school? I believe the best way to get you all caught up on your credits is to do it through a homeschool forum. That is, if you are okay with it."

Ki piped up and said, "Man, I wish you would have homeschooled me. I hated high school."

Rose laughed, "I wasn't old enough to retire then, but nothing's stopping me now."

Halee didn't say anything about hating school. I think she's more of a social butterfly than Ki. That's my impression anyway.

"Well, Eva. What do you think?" asked Ed.

"I-I don't know what to say. I hate high school."

Everyone smiled, and Ki said, "You will love being homeschooled."

"I thought a portion of the day could be spent on traditional bookwork and learning, another portion could be used to let you focus on journaling, you could have some free time to do whatever you wanted, and we could rotate days between counseling with Dr. Lydia and an art program. I thought you would enjoy that. I know you like to draw. Does this sound like something you would be interested in?"

"Would I have to take art at the high school?" I asked.

"No, hon. I'd like to enroll you in a community art program. I think you'd enjoy it more. They also have a therapeutic art program I thought about."

"Oh good. I don't want to go back to that high school after Ian," I said.

"I don't blame you. This will be much better for you anyway. You can focus on the things you really enjoy," replied Rose.

"Once you have a certain number of high school credits, you can start taking classes through the community college."

"Really? I can take college classes in high school," I sputtered in amazement.

"You can. You're smart enough to pass the classes now, but you don't have all the required credits. We'll get all of that taken care of sooner than later though," said Rose.

"Oh wow! I can't wait!" I exclaimed.

"Are college classes a lot harder than high school classes?" I asked staring directly at Halee.

"Not really. They're a little harder, but they're so much better and are so much more interesting. The basic math, English, and the undergraduate pre-requisites are boring, but then you get to focus on your major," Halee promised.

Rose interjected, "Eva, when the time is right, I will explain all of that stuff to you. For now, you just need to know that it can happen."

I must have been grinning from ear-to-ear because my face literally started to hurt from smiling so much.

Leaving for Melissa's house now.

I'll write more later,

Eva

Dear Kami,

Melissa was happy about Rose helping me with my goals. She was proud of me for opening-up and asking for help.

She loved my new outfit.

I can't wait to show her my new bedroom digs! I know she'll like them. She'll be surprised I didn't choose black bedding. She told me she was surprised my new outfit wasn't black. I told her I think I'm done with that phase. She said, "I'm glad. You're way too pretty to ignore all the colorful clothing out there. You look like a new you."

I laughed, "Yeah, I feel like a new me. Thanks for getting me hooked up with the Paxton's. They are such good people. They're so real. I think they really like me."

Melissa did that obvious throat clearing thing and said, "Eva, they more than like you. They absolutely adore you. Literally, they love you."

"I don't know why I ended up getting so lucky when there are so many kids out there who never do," I sighed.

"Don't over analyze it. It's your time for something truly wonderful to happen. You deserve it; you've been through so much. You deserve all the best and so much more. I am glad you are letting them treat you well. It sounds like you guys are really hitting it off. I was worried you may not open up to them, but I've been proven wrong, which is awesome! You couldn't be joining a better family. They can't wait until you move in with them."

I didn't respond. I just sat in silence with a smile on my face. It feels so nice to be wanted. So nice!

"Melissa, how long do you think I will have to go to counseling with Dr. Lydia?" I asked.

"At least through your final adoption. Why? Do you not like her?" she asked.

"I do. I just wonder if I will have to go to counseling forever," I said.

"Maybe not forever, but certainly long term. Like many, many years. If you want to find someone besides Dr. Lydia, we can work on that, but not until the adoption goes through."

"I just don't like going back to the hospital, and I know once I get discharged, I'll never want to go back."

"I don't think that will be a problem, Eva. And, you may want to be in some form of therapy your entire life. It sure is nice to have an objective person to bounce ideas off sometimes. There are many people who cut their sessions back to once a month when they feel settled and have some resolution in their lives. Once a month would be good as a maintenance kind of thing. Ya know?"

"We're here already?" I winced.

"Hang in there and keep focused on your goals. I can't stress that enough. You'll be out soon enough. Don't rush it. You're doing so well. Trust me. Just go with the flow. Rose and Ed are working diligently on their end to make this happen as soon as possible."

I smiled, waved, and set off to check in with the white coats.

Toting my heavy bag, I realized I wouldn't be toting a bag next time because I already have everything I need at the Paxton's. I have my own clothes, pj's, slippers, shoes, toothbrush, and minimalist bedding.

And my thoughts land with Harry. I bet he would be proud of my shopping accomplishments this weekend. I hope he is okay!

They just rang the dinner bell. I'll go find Billy and Olivia. I hope the food is good tonight.

TTYL,

Eva

Dear Kami,

I'm stopping in for a quick time out, so I can have ten minutes alone. Dr. Lydia just told me I'll only have one more weekend visit with the Paxton's.

Because I'll be living with them by the following weekend!!!

I'm on top of the world! Dr. Lydia said she would let me handle making the announcement.

She asked me for my journals, so she could review my goals. I told her I hadn't completed two of them, and she said that was fine and we'd get to them.

She also asked me to start thinking about taking the Paxton family name, or not. Wow, that's something I hadn't considered. I have group in three minutes.

Gotta run,

Eva

Dear Kami,

Group was rough. I don't mask my emotions very well, and Mother Olivia was on me like stink-on-shit. She's Dr. Lydia's assistant and takes her role seriously.

"Eva, you look like you're somewhere else. Is there anything you want to talk about?" she said, calling me out in front of everyone.

"Actually, yes. I was going to wait because I just found out and I haven't had time to process it, but I'll be leaving here in two weeks. Next weekend will be my last home visit with the Paxton's and then I'll be moving in with them soon after that," I said in one huge exhaled breath.

And, with that, Dr. Lydia took the floor, "We are all very proud of Eva and need to tell her what we like and appreciate about her. I'd like everyone to participate. Eva, you get to respond to each member by also telling them one thing you like and appreciate about them. Olivia, why don't you take the lead? Please tell Eva what you like and appreciate about her."

Just like that, the pregnancy hormones took over. She was a babbling mess. "Eva, you've been such a good friend to me. I want to be the kind of person you are. If I can do that, I'll be a great mom, the kind my baby needs. I am really going to miss you. I hope we keep in touch," whispered Olivia in a failed attempt not to cry.

"Good job, Olivia. Eva, why don't you tell Olivia what you like and appreciate about her," Dr. Lydia prompted.

"Okay, so here goes. Olivia, you are a great friend to everybody. You're a natural leader and you're very pretty," I managed to say without shedding a tear.

"Great work. Billy, why don't you go next," said Dr. Lydia.

"Eva, you were the first person to be nice to me here. You were my first friend. You are a very nice person. I hope you have a nice life," he muttered.

I piped up, "Billy, you'll never understand how much you helped me. I will never forget you, the hot chocolate, or the fire. You are always here for me when I need help. I am going to miss you a lot."

"Thank you, Billy and Eva. Frankie, it's your turn. Please tell Eva what you like and appreciate about her," said Dr. Lydia.

"Um . . . Well, I don't like her, so what do you want me to say?" Frankie spat.

"Since you are choosing to be defiant, you will sit here until you come up with one thing you appreciate about her. You don't have to like her. I highly suspect she isn't a fan of Frankie Sanders either," replied Dr. Lydia.

That earned a chuckle from everyone.

"I appreciate the fact that she's leaving soon," Frankie said.

"One more rude remark and you'll lose all privileges," replied Dr. Lydia.

"Whatever," yelled Frankie.

"Get outta here now! Go back to your room," Dr. Lydia instructed.

"Are you okay Eva?" she continued.

"I'm fine. I don't care if she likes me or not. I don't like her either," I replied.

"Okay. It's my turn. I appreciate your spirit of survival and I like your heart. You are a true survivor and I am happy to know you," Dr. Lydia urged.

"Dr. Lydia, you forced me to do the hard work of really looking and thinking about my shit.

No one has ever pushed my boundaries like you do. Thank you for helping me," I tearily replied.

And, with that, Olivia clapped her hands signaling the end of group. She came up and bear hugged me like I've never been bear hugged before.

Love,

Eva

Dear Kami,

Olivia bursts out in tears like every fifteen minutes since she found out I'm leaving. I told her we can write letters and visit when she gets out. I doubt I'll have a whole lot of free time though. Between my high school credits and college classes, I think I'll be very busy. I keep thinking about what Dr. Lydia said about taking the Paxton family name. I've never thought about not being Eva Langston.

Eva Paxton . . .

That doesn't sound bad, but I like having the same last name as Mama.

Eva Paxton . . .

I wonder if Rose and Ed would be upset if I didn't take their name? I've been Eva Langston for almost seventeen years. Maybe I'll ask Melissa what she thinks. She always has good advice. I trust her judgment.

Rose and Ed have been so good to me, I hope they don't mind.

And, just like that, my thoughts are interrupted. The white coats stopped by to let me know Dr. Lydia is ready to meet with me. I'll write more later this evening.

Got a busy rest-of-the-afternoon,

Eva

Dear Kami,

The first thing Dr. Lydia asked me about was the Paxton family name. I hesitated, "I--I think…". Dr. Lydia interjected, "Eva, it is okay to keep your last name. The Paxton's are fine either way. They just wanted you to have a choice. And, they need to know for all the legal paperwork. Relax! This is one thing you can stop thinking about."

I exhaled, "Oh, that makes me feel better. I didn't want to disappoint them."

"You won't, Eva. They really don't seem to mind," she replied.

"I am amazed with the amount of work you put into documenting your goals. You've done an incredible amount of work in a relatively small amount of time. I am impressed by your willingness to reach out and ask for help when you've needed it. I have high hopes for your future and I know you'll be successful in achieving your goals. You are a resilient and strong young woman. You've acquired some useful basic skills that will help you through difficult times. You *will* have some difficult times. Everyone does… How you handle difficulties is what matters. I have faith the Paxton's will be great guides for you throughout the rest of this crazy maze we call life," she continued.

I don't know, but it sure seemed like a weight was lifted from my shoulders when Dr. Lydia told me the Paxton's were fine with me keeping my last name. I like the name Paxton, but I'm a Langston.

Dr. Lydia also brought up counseling once I'm released. I'll meet with her twice a week until the adoption is finalized, and once per week after unless I need to continue seeing her two times a week. The good news is that once the adoption is finalized, Dr. Lydia wants to move our counseling appointments to her private practice office. That means I will not have to return to this depressing hospital anymore once I'm officially adopted. She said because I'm a ward of the state, my appointments have to be at the hospital for insurance reasons.

Everything is falling into place!

Mama would be so happy for me. She'd say I deserve to live in that big ole' fancy house and to have nice things. She always wanted the best for me, even through her struggles. She would be so proud of how smart I am and how much I've learned. She's the one who taught me to read, write, and do math. I'm still not very good at math and have a lot of catch-up work to do, but I'm good at most other subjects.

Rose said she would hire a special tutor to help me with math. She said she will also help, but wants to approach it from a few angles in-case I learn better with one person's style versus another's.

Dinner time.

TTYL,

Eva

Dear Kami,

Well, D--day is finally here! Departure day . . . I can't wait!

I am leaving a couple of my new outfits with Olivia. They will fit her once she has the baby. At least that way she'll have a couple of nice things to wear.

I already made my rounds and said goodbye to everyone.

I'm waiting for Rose and Ed to come pick me up. I'm a little early, but I'm excited. I'm supposed to meet them in the lobby at one o'clock and its noon.

And . . . I'm left with my thoughts.

I wonder if the newness will wear off and they'll get sick of me?

I wonder if I'll be a huge disappointment to them?

How will I stack up to Ki and Halee?

And, just like that, I see their car pulling in. They're early too!

I'd love to run out and meet them, but until I'm officially discharged, I can't walk through the front doors without an escort.

With knots in my stomach, I wait. I'll write more later.

I can't wait to see them,

Eva

Dear Kami,

I had the best day! Rose and Ed planned a surprise party for me and invited Melissa, Ki, and Halee. We grilled hamburgers, hotdogs, and had cake and ice cream.

Rose got another rug just like the one I picked out that is beside my bed and she already put it under the bed for me!

I am very lucky. I have a Mama who loves me and a new family who is already fond of me. Melissa says they love me already. I know I like them a lot. I like them more than you just like a friend. Melissa said it may take me some time to learn to love again. And, to fully trust. All I know is that I am very lucky and have a way cool new family.

Rose and Ed want to have family photos made. They asked if I am okay with that. I have never done a family portrait before. I think it will be nice. Rose said the not-so-fun part will be coordinating a time that also fits into Ki and Halee's schedules.

Rose has all the home school classes set up already, but she said she wants to give me about a week to settle in before we begin. I told her I'm ready for my classes because I want to get caught up, but she insisted. She said transition periods are important. She promised we'd get caught up in no time. It's so nice to be part of a *we* again.

I'm ready to crawl under my bed and try out the new rug. Going to catch some ZZZ's.

TTYL,

Eva

Dear Kami,

Wow! My classes are going amazingly well and I'm loving them!

Home school is so much better than dealing with the dreadful and crazy world of public high school. I feel like I can be myself and not always be on the defense. High school kids are so mean, and everyone walks around like the living dead. It's like they're robots and are programmed to live and act exactly as they think their peers want them to.

I understand why Ian went mad. I really do. I don't agree with what he was planning, but I understand the reason behind it.

I turned seventeen a few months ago and in no way fit in with the kids at my old school. I don't fit in with the younger ones or the older ones. Rose says it's because I've had more life experience that most forty-year-olds. She said I've had some really bad and traumatic experiences and is proud of the way I've come through them. She's proud of me for working through a lot of my anger and sadness too. I still get depressed sometimes, but I haven't thought about killing myself in a long time. Well, long time in my world, lol.

Rose thinks I'll be caught up and ready to graduate in two and a half years. I'll be pushing twenty! I thought I would be done sooner. That includes taking some college classes too though. I guess I did smoke a lot of pot and skip classes way too much to be on track.

It doesn't matter anyway. It's not like I have friends that I'll miss graduating with. Rose says the most important thing is how well I learn what I'm supposed to learn, not how fast. I guess that makes sense. I just hate math! I struggle with it even with a tutor, but at least I try. I love reading and writing. I could do both all day long.

I start my first art therapy class tomorrow. It's really just an art class, but Rose said spinning clay is one of the most therapeutic things you can do. I'm excited about that. She's going to take the class with me because she loves working with clay. I will be in the beginner class, and she'll be in the intermediate section. It's during the day when most kids will be in school, thank God! Rose said some other homeschool kids will likely be there. I'm trying to be brave. I don't always do so well meeting new people.

Rose wanted to enroll me in swim lessons at the community pool. That is a place where many homeschooled kids go with their parents for exercise and a break in their school day.

I had a panic attack Rose helped me through. She said we can put swim lessons on the back burner for now and will re-visit it in a few months. She wants me to learn to swim for my own safety. I get it! It's just the thought of other kids watching me learn how to swim that makes me nervous. The lady who used to teach private and semi-private lessons retired. They haven't replaced her yet. I think I'd rather take a private or semi-private lesson.

Back to the books! I used my free time to do some journaling.

I miss you, Kami,

Eva

Dear Kami,

School is still going well. I love the art class! You can do so much with clay.

Ernie, an older man in the class has taken me under his wing and shares his techniques with me. He is in the intermediate class, but makes time to help me.

I sometimes day dream and wonder if this is what having a grandpa is like. I never met Mama's mother or father; she wasn't close to them. She ran away from home when she was fifteen and hasn't seen them since.

And, there's China. I think she's cute. I would call her style unusual and hippy. She wears these long, flowing skirts, and Birkenstocks. I love her dreadlocks! She makes my stomach turn flips. Literally...

I don't think she even knows I exist. I dream about her patchouli oil perfume. I am not usually a fan of patchouli oil, but I swear, *she* makes *it* smell good!

I've been in class for three months and China has never as much as looked my way, our eyes have never met, and, nope, I'm pretty sure she doesn't even know I exist.

Ernie caught me eying her and said, "You know, you could just go introduce yourself." I blushed and shook my head no.

I usually have pretty good "gay-dar," but something is telling me China doesn't want to be disturbed. So, I don't.

My dreams at night fall on China. Not the country, but the girl. The beautiful girl I am crazy about. In my dream, our eyes lock in class and we blush. She casually walks up to me, traces my red face with her long fingers, and tucks my wild locks behind my ears. I return to the bowl I am spinning. China follows and sits directly behind me. The warmth of her body pressed against my back makes my heart rush. Her hands lace through mine and we let the clay and wetness ooze through our fingers. The blend of patchouli and cigarettes wafts through her hair.

My dream immediately startles me awake, and I think of Ian. He smoked Marlboro cigarettes. I wonder how he is doing, and doze back off.

In what seemed like only minutes later, I am greeting the morning courtesy of my insanely loud alarm clock. I've never slept so soundly in my life. Since I've had this bed and comfy bedding, I've slept through four alarms. Rose finally bought an alarm clock that is not only super loud, it vibrates my bed. Yes, it vibrates my entire bed.

No sleeping through that beast!

Ta-ta for now,

Eva

Dear Kami,

I haven't seen China in art class in over three weeks. I asked the instructor if she dropped out, and she said she hadn't heard from her. Ahhh, my teenage heart breaks.

During a break from my studies, Rose asked me about you. I hold her you were my best friend and were always there for me when I needed you.

"Was she a neighbor?" she continued.

"Sort-of. I never saw her house and there were no real neighbors close to us," I replied.

"Was she the same age as you?" she asked.

"I never really thought about it," I semi-whispered, my voice cracking.

With a knowing smile, Rose softly replied, "I had a friend like that when I was young too. She helped me through many tough situations, including my parents' divorce. Kami sounds delightful. I'm glad you have such a wonderful friend." And, that was it. No more talk about it.

Rose shifted the conversation onto swim lessons. "I found a lady who gives private swim lessons out of her home. I would love it if you would consider the lessons," she mused.

"I think I am ready now. I don't feel scared anymore. I will try my best to learn to swim and be brave," I promised.

With that, she smiled and went into the kitchen to make us both an afternoon snack. Stuffing my face with apples and peanut butter!

Will write later,

Eva

Dear Kami,

Since the conclusion of the pottery class, I've begun swim lessons and signed up for another art class, watercolor for beginners. Rose doesn't share the same interest and isn't taking this class with me. Instead, she's taking an advanced pottery class, way beyond my skill level.

I am getting more comfortable in the water. I can now tread water and dog-paddle. At least I know I wouldn't drown if I fell into deep water. I understand Rose's insistence on me taking lessons, I really do.

I like Marilyn; she's a great instructor. I know I'll never swim as gracefully as she, but swimming like a swan has never really been my goal. I simply wanted to learn how to swim, not be a rock star.

My adoption is final at last, so I'll be able to start seeing Dr. Lydia at her private practice location. Yay! She helped me break the news of my sexual orientation to Rose and Ed. They were about as concerned by the news as they would be by me saying I'm taking a shower. They clearly didn't care and told me they were proud of me for being brave and trusting enough to tell them.

Also, since the adoption is final, I'll be able to visit Olivia. She and her baby were placed in a therapeutic foster home. We've been emailing back and forth and skyping. Rose is taking me to visit her this weekend.

We'll all go to lunch somewhere; I'll ask Olivia to choose the place.

Exhausted!

Going to catch some ZZZ's,

Eva

Dear Kami,

The visit with Olivia was fine, I guess. We don't seem to have the same connection anymore. Our conversation felt strained. Not sure if we'll hang out again… The only thing we have in common is the mental hospital, and that's something I want to put behind me.

Rose senses the change in my mood during our ride home and asks, "Are you okay?"

I sigh, "Yes, I'm just sad. Every time I make a friend, something happens, and the friendship ends. I know Olivia and I are very different, but our conversation was even difficult this time."

"True and lasting friendship takes time. Olivia is now a mother, so many of her struggles are going to be different than yours. And, there's the molestation by her foster father that will always be the elephant in the room. She will not be able to escape it, as she bore the child he fathered. She may regret her decision not to place the child up for adoption. I'm sure she noticed how much you have also changed. I suspect she's envious. You have made great strides. Your physical appearance has even changed. You look like a happy person, smiley and more confident. Your school progress alone would be enough to make her doubt herself," she replied.

"She deserves to be happy too. I just don't think us hanging out again will make either of us happy," I muttered.

"Friendship will happen. Don't be in a hurry. High school is difficult; the age is difficult. I believe you will meet more mature people and will make friends when you start junior college. Most people are there because they need to be there, and want to be there. Four-year schools are often a different beast, and many students are only there because their parents made them go, and because their parents paid for them to be there. I think you will enjoy junior college. From there, you can always transfer to a four-year school," she urged.

"What would you think about me going to an art school?" I asked

Smiling, Rose said, "I think that sounds like something that would be right up your alley. Are you interested in any particular medium?"

"I've been thinking a lot about the glass blowing class I took. I'm hooked! Like you with clay, I love working with glass. I've been researching programs," I said with a returned smile.

"Tell ya what! We'll make time tomorrow to sit down together and see what's out there, K?" Rose promised.

"Thank you," I replied.

And, we're home.

TTYL,

Eva

Dear Kami,

I can't believe Rose, Ed, Halee, Ki, and I are going to Hawaii! This trip will mark many firsts for me. It will be my first time on a plane and my first time out of the continental United States.

I am still a little scared, but Rose promised me we'll be fine. She wants me to take a motion sickness pill before the flight, just in case.

Halee and Ki have flown all over the world. They both studied abroad in high school and in college.

The main purpose of the trip is to take a tour of the University of Hawaii at Manoa. UH is Rose's alma mater and she said they have a magnificent art program. She wants to show me around the campus and have me meet with an advisor.

She said she's excited to hike many of the beautiful forests and can't wait to show off her favorite waterfall and swim spot.

Since pineapple is one of my favorite fruits, we'll tour the Dole pineapple plantation while we're there; I can't wait!

We're renting a house in the Diamond Head area.

Ki and Halee are excited about surfing, but I ensured them I wouldn't be trying it. They used to vacation in Hawaii often when Ki and Halee were younger. That's how they learned to surf. I think I'll stick to snorkeling in shallow water. I'm not into sharks and fish so large they can bite off your leg with one chomp.

School is going better than expected and I should graduate in about a year.

I've taken all the glass blowing classes I can find and am still in love. I'd love to go to France one day to study under one of the greats.

I haven't seen Melissa much lately because she and Justen are planning their wedding. They have been engaged for three months now. I understand her being busy with work and having a wedding to plan. She asked me to make cream and white colored blown glass ornaments to hang from the arbor Justen is making for their wedding photos. I've already made half of them; it's such a blast! She isn't paying me, but she is paying for the material and my use of the equipment. I don't care about not being paid. I'm just having fun!

I better go and get started packing. We leave in about a week and a half.

Rose wants me to take a break from my studies while we're on vacation. I'm certainly not going to argue. She wants me to keep journaling, however. I like journaling. I can see keeping a journal forever.

My hand is getting tired though. Time for a break and to start packing!

Later,

Eva

Dear Kami,

The flight was almost uneventful. A drunk man was escorted off the plane by officers wearing plain clothes. He was slurring his speech and kicking his feet. I got a whiff of puke as they dragged him past me. It was a horrid scent. I wonder if he puked on the plane or puked on another passenger? I'm just glad we weren't seated next to him! Other than the drunk man episode, all was well.

I didn't take any more motion sickness medicine because I could tell I wouldn't need it; I did fine. My ears popped every now and then, but Halee showed me how to unplug them by holding my nose and blowing out, not letting air escape. And, it worked!

When we landed we were greeted with lays in-hand. Ki looked at me and squealed, "You've finally been lei'd! How'd it feel?"

I just smiled and thought, *what you don't know won't kill you.* All five of us were lei'd. The property manager of the vacation house we rented in Diamond Head greeted us upon arrival at the Honolulu International Airport with our rental car, keys to the house, and lays.

We were all bushed, so Rose suggested we unpack and take a nap before we set off to explore.

I couldn't believe my eyes when we arrived! Rose and Ed shared a bedroom, but Ki, Halee, and I had our own bedrooms with en suite bathrooms.

The backyard was to die for! It had the most interesting looking swimming pool I'd ever seen. Ed called it a lap pool and said that's how he planned to spend his mornings before breakfast. Swimming laps!

Going to take a nap!

TTYL,

Eva

Dear Kami,

When I woke from my nap, I wandered around the house and made my way to the backyard. Everyone was sitting around a large rectangular wooden table. Ed saw me and waved, "Hey, sleepy-head! I thought you were going to sleep the afternoon away. Come try these delicious orange slices. They're dipped in chocolate!"

And, they were amazing! Just two years ago, trying fruit dipped in chocolate would have been out of the question, or at least a struggle. But, I've managed to keep my promise to continue trying new foods, and amazingly, I like most of them!

"The property management company left these on the kitchen counter for us. Aren't they spectacular?" Rose said as she savored the sweetness on her lips.

"Eva, take-a-look over there," said Ki.

"Are those grapefruit trees?" I asked.

"They sure are! And they look ripe. Let's try one," suggested Ki.

Halee, Ki, and I picked the plumpest fruit we could find. Rose made a mad dash to the kitchen for a knife and cutting board. Ki cut the round fruit into five equally sized wedges. I put the beauty in between my lips and could have almost had an orgasm, literally. It was heavenly! It sent a tingling feeling from the sourness combined with the sweet up into my nose. My eyes watered! I know what I'll be eating a lot of while I am here!

On day two, on our way to UH to meet with an advisor and take a tour of the campus, we stopped by the Honolulu Chocolate Company and scored some chocolate dipped macadamia nuts. Another first! I'd never tried macadamia nuts.

These were sure to top the charts as one of my favorite nuts. OMG! The man behind the counter smiled as he watched my eyes roll back as I sampled heaven. If there is a heaven, I'm sure these salty, sweet treats will be there too. Wow!

I can't imagine anyone not liking Hawaii!

We met with Dr. Kealoha at 9 a.m. He explained that his last name meant the loved one, combining two very traditional Hawaiian words. Aloha means love and Ke is a definite article (coming before k, e, a, or o).

He now lives on Oahu but was born and raised on Moloka'i where he learned to spear fish as a young boy. He suggested we give it a try while we're here. He said the Moi fish are plentiful this time of year. He also suggested sailing out to Lanai for the best snorkeling around. Both sound like fun to me!

Rose begun by sharing my foster care history, enough to give him insight but not enough to make me uncomfortable.

Dr. Kealoha went over some of the basic admission requirements and asked if we would like a guided tour when Rose piped up and said, "Oh no, that's okay. I can show her the ropes."

He smiled, "Of course you can, Rose."

She smiled back and thanked him.

As we walked out I asked, "What was that about? You know him?"

She smiled, "He dated my roommate in college. I've known him for a very long time."

"Why didn't you tell me he was your friend?" I asked curiously.

"Honestly, I didn't really think about it. We're not close and we hadn't spoken in many years until I set up this appointment."

I just smiled. I thought about what Rose would have been like in college. I bet most of the boys liked her; she's so sweet and is very pretty.

Our tour lasted about an hour. I was overwhelmed by the huge campus. Rose said she was overwhelmed when she started too, but promised I'd feel comfortable in no time at all.

We stopped by the International Market Place on the way back to the rental house. Rose smiled as she pulled in and said, "Oh wow, it's been remodeled. It looks great! Eva, you're gonna love this place!"

And, I did!

Halee rushed to get seating at the Flour & Barley pizza place. The line was out the door. If there's one thing I've learned about the Paxton's, it's that they all love pizza. I tolerate it and usually stick with cheese pizza.

Although I ordered cheese, I tried a slice of Ki's shrimp pizza and loved it! I will order that next time!

Rose kept smiling at me while we were eating.

I finally asked, "What gives?"

She softly replied, "We are all so proud of all you've accomplished and overcome. You have gone through so much in your life."

I smiled and quickly realized I had pizza sauce stuck in my teeth, so I made my way to the bathroom to fix the problem.

We bought fish from a local market and made grilled fish, mango salsa, and a baked potato for dinner. The mango salsa wasn't my thing, but the fish and potato were both tasty! I'm zonked.

Going to bed,

Eva

Dear Kami,

Laniakea Beach was a blast! Halee and Ki are great with a surf board! Rose got some great shots of them on the waves.

I love snorkeling! There were so many sea turtles out today. They're huge!

I have never seen so many colorful fish in my life. They swim right past you and seem un-phased by people. I almost had a heart attack when I thought I saw a shark. It wasn't. Instead, it was some other medium-sized, shark-looking, fish.

Rose and Ed also enjoyed snorkeling and pointing out various coral reef stacks.

I found a strange-looking creature in the water; it looked like a soggy, exotic cucumber. Rose said it was, in fact, a sea cucumber. Little did I know!

We had such a great time until I ruined it all . . . . . .

Yes . . . Me . . . The Idiot . . .

We were walking up the beach heading back to the car when we passed a group of homeless people camping on the beach. I thought I saw Mama and started running towards her yelling, "Mama, Mama! It's me, Eva!"

Rose tried to hold me back warning, "Honey, it's not her."

I broke free of the firm grip she had on my arm and ran up to you with open arms. I hugged you with tears pouring down my cheeks until you pushed me away. A nearby local witnessed the account and yelled, "Stupid Haole!"

Rose ran up to me and wrapped me in her arms. She was weeping and sobbing loudly. I've never seen her yell at anyone, but she looked over at the local and screamed, "Get the hell outta here, you asshole!"

And, he did.

I think he was afraid because she donned a crazy look in her eyes.

Ki and Halee were also bawling. They ran over and embraced Rose and me.

Ed stood back, almost like he was a prison guard protecting us from the goons.

The drive back to the rental house was quiet. Dead quiet.

When we reached the house, everyone peeled out, still silent.

I made my way to the room I was sleeping in and crawled into bed. I heard the door creak and Rose slinked in quietly. She didn't knock like she normally did. She simply slid in bed behind me and held me in her arms. We both fell asleep.

When we woke, Rose whispered, "I am so sorry about today. I wish things would have happened differently. I don't like to see you hurting; it tears me apart. I know you would like to see your Mom again. I know I will never replace her, and I don't wish to. There is no competition. I love and cherish you and want all the happiness in the world for you. Ed and I discussed hiring a private investigator to try to find her. We've never felt the timing was right and didn't want to overstep our bounds. I think the time has come. Is this something you want?"

Bawling again, "Yes, please. But, wouldn't it be expensive to hire an investigator?"

"Yes, baby girl. It would be expensive, but I believe it would be worth it. Ed and I would call it your graduation gift from us," said Rose softly.

"I think you're ready. For closure, I mean. Closure to the unknowing and uncertainty. Not closure to your relationship with your Mom. We hope she will be a part of your life forever if she can be a healthy influence. If not, we believe you are mature and stable enough to understand limitations," she continued.

"I am ready," I promised.

We lay there for a few short moments before Ed knocked on the door, "You two okay in there?"

I answered, "Yes," and Ed opened the door with Halee and Ki following.

"I am sorry I screwed up our perfect day," I said.

"Are you serious? You didn't screw anything up! Our beach day was perfect," said Halee as she dog-piled on top of Rose and I. Ki started laughing and said, "Halee, you're a freak! Get off them! They can't breathe!"

With that, Ed extended his hands and helped Halee, Rose, and I up, one after the other.

Rose smiled, looked at Ed and said, "It's time."

Ed smiled and said, "I figured."

He didn't even hesitate. Apparently, they had been talking a lot about it.

Halee squealed, "Ki and I want to meet her too!"

Ed replied, "Okay, but you need to give Eva her time first."

"I think she would love you guys," I replied.

With that, we headed to the kitchen for a hunt-and-pick dinner.

Later,

Eva

Dear Kami,

Before we left Hawaii, we took Dr. Kealoha's advice and went spear fishing on Molokai and snorkeling on Lanai. It turns out that I have quite a knack for spearfishing. I speared six Moi, Ki got two, Halee and Ed got one, and Rose got a big fat zero.

With our moods high and our luck even better, we sailed over to Lanai where beautiful fish after fish swam by. Their fins and fancy colors were on display like they were auditioning for a Broadway play. I'd never seen anything so amazing!

We hurried back to the rental, anxious to try the Moi we'd speared. We were all exhausted. We baked the delicious Moi and served it with brown rice. That was our last dinner in Hawaii.

I've since begun the application process for UH. I can't stop dreaming about her, about Hawaii. Her beauty, her stamina, and her magic.

A magic that pulls you in and enfolds you in her warmth.

My studies are now at best, mundane, and I am ready to graduate. I am ready to carve out the next phase of my life.

Rose and Ed hired a private investigator to search for Mama. He hasn't produced any real leads, but I'm not giving up hope. I know she's alive! I want her to be proud of me. I want her to like Rose, Ed, Halee, and Ki.

I want them to like her, not in a kum-by-ah sense, but in a she did the best she could sense. I know she has her issues and could have done so many things differently, but she didn't. She did what she thought was best at the time. I know she loved me.

If I am not accepted into UH's art program, I' don't know what I'll do. I guess there's always the Academy of Arts College in San Francisco, although I'm not really a fan of San Francisco. I'd probably have to live on anti-anxiety medicine if I chose to go to school there. Just the sheer volume of people and the crowds would send my head spinning. So, I guess that really isn't an option.

I don't really have a Plan B, so I hope my Plan A works out!

I think it's about time I have another visit with Dr. Lydia. She always helps me process and work through the jumbled thoughts in my head.

I don't know why I feel so unsettled right now. But, I do.

I'll write more later,

Eva

I think it's about time I have another visit with Dr. Lydia. She always helps me process and work through the jumbled thoughts in my head.

Dear Kami,

As always, my time with Dr. Lydia helped me make sense of the mess I call life. I told her how I ran up to a woman on the beach in Hawaii I thought was mama; I told her about how I had no Plan B, and I told her about Rose and Ed hiring a private investigator to try to find Mama.

She told me a story about her actually believing she saw her deceased brother driving up the road. She made an illegal U-turn on a busy road, almost hit another car, and followed her brother's ghost. She said she knew logically he was dead, but her heart rushed logic out the door. When she finally caught up to the ghost, she was crushed, realizing it wasn't him. She began shaking and sobbing uncontrollably and pulled off the road to process what she'd just done.

She explained that just because one's current situation precludes them from seeing or spending time with someone doesn't mean you stop loving them and hoping. I didn't feel so bad about my embarrassing display of idiocy after that.

She is glad Rose and Ed have the resources and are willing to help me find Mama. She wants me to prepare myself for any possible outcome including death, drug addiction, homelessness, joblessness, living with someone, acting as a co-parent to a child, etc.... I'd never considered the possibility that she could have another child or be a step parent to someone else's. I don't know how I'd feel about that. It would make me wonder why she never tried to find me, I know that much for sure!

I'm prepared for drug abuse and homelessness because that's what I've been led to believe for so long. Finding out she was dead would be another ground shaking piece of news. It would shatter any hope I had of building a future relationship with her, obviously. It would also make me tremendously sad. I'd wonder how she died, if she was in pain, and if she died alone.

I'd wonder if she thought about me before taking her last breath.

Dr. Lydia wants me to craft a fictitious scripted conversation with her for each of those situations, excluding death, obviously. She said that would help me stay grounded even if I decided not to use any portion of the script. Sounds like hooey to me, but Dr. Lydia has never led me astray, so it's something I will focus on before our next appointment.

As far as not having a Plan B, she doesn't think it's likely a life-ender. She said she believes I can get into any art program I apply to. She also reminded me there are less traditional programs, including non-degree programs. I'd thought about attending something like that, but only after going to college and earning a four-year degree. I'd be the first person in my family to go to college. Of course, I don't know anything about my biological father's family.

Before I left her office, she said, "Eva, you've got this!" *That* made me smile so big it hurt!

Rose just rang the dinner bell.

TTYL,

Eva

Dear Kami,

I'm still bumbling along in my classes and am wishing I were already done. Oh, how I'd love to call myself a high school graduate!

The perks of having a family who cares for me is beyond anything I could have ever dreamed of. Literally.

Rose told me the private investigator believes he may have a lead on Mama. He's flying out to Las Vegas, Nevada to follow up on the lead and will let us know as soon as he knows anything more. It would be so great to see her, if only for a short visit. She'd be amazed at how much I've grown up and changed. She always wanted me to be smart; she would be proud! I can't wait to tell her my plan to attend U.H.

Yes, yes, yes, I finished the scripts like Dr. Lydia asked me to, although I hope I won't need them. I hope Mama will be just fine.

Rose recently asked me if I would like to study to take my driver's license test. I don't know. In Hawaii, I probably won't be driving much anyway. Most students walk, ride scooters, or take public transportation. I told her I'd think about it.

She said it's a skill everyone should at least have in case of an emergency. She's probably right, like she was about the swim lessons. I just never really imagined myself driving. Cars are so dangerous. We see wrecks almost every time we leave the house, and people drive so fast!

I don't know.

I don't know.

I don't know.

I will consider it though. For Rose...

Going to take a nap under my bed,

Eva

Dear Kami,

Damn it! The private investigator said he found a halfway house where Mama used to live, up until about three weeks ago. Apparently, she failed a routine drug screening for the third time in a row and was kicked out. They said they didn't have a forwarding address for her or a last known address. She tested positive for methamphetamine.

The private investigator searched areas in Vegas known to attract the homeless such as the bridges connecting casinos, churches, soup kitchens, rehabs, county jail, and other halfway houses. There are no formal homeless shelters in

Vegas apparently, so that wasn't an option. It's as if she were a ghost.

If she's into drugs and owes a debt, I guess she'd have to get good at disappearing.

I wonder if the mere thought of her will ever be less intoxicating for me?

Rose keeps checking in with me to make sure I'm okay since we received the news. She knows how much I was hoping for good news. The truth is, I am fine. I am more than fine because I'm still here. I don't think about killing myself anymore, I'm almost a high school graduate, I have a family whose absolutely nuts about me, and I have a biological mom, as dysfunctional as she may be, who's still alive and out there, somewhere.

I mean, really. Things could be way worse. I could be dead, I could have never met Rose, Ed, Halee, and Ki, I could be pregnant, and I could have dropped out of high school. But nope, that's not my story. Thank god!

Feeling like I need some family time!

I will write more later,

Eva

Dear Kami,

Melissa came over for a visit. She, Rose, Ed, and I played several rounds of Apples to Apples and Code Names. Those are two of my favorite games; I could play for hours. Ummm, I did play for hours! Lol.

Melissa finally had to stop playing because she said she had a list of wedding chores to complete. She said she was happy to have a short break from all the wedding to-do's. I don't blame her!

If I ever get married, I know I don't want a huge wedding. It seems like so much drama and stress for what?

I've finally decided to take the written driver's license test, so I can get my permit. Rose taught Halee and Ki to drive. She says she's excited to teach me too. She knows I'm nervous but insists I'll do fine. I guess . . .

She promises we'll start slow, in a deserted parking lot or something similar. Her car has a manual transmission, so she and Ed will switch cars on the days I practice. I want to learn using a car with an automatic transmission. That will at least cut out some of the fluff. I think I'll be too overwhelmed for a manual anyway.

Time for a snack! Going to try the crab and artichoke dip Melissa made because I promised I would. I'm still not a huge fan of concoctions with several ingredients in them, but I can't say I don't like what I'm unwilling to try.

Will write later,

Eva

Dear Kami,

The study guide to take the driver's permit exam is so simple a six-year-old could pass it. Well, maybe not a six-year-old, but certainly a twelve-year-old.

I'm scheduled to take the written exam later this week. I have no doubt I'll pass. The written portion isn't what worries me. It's the driving part. Rose promises we'll go slow, and I trust her, so I know I'll be fine. I'm just nervous, that's all.

Rose checked the mail and placed a thick envelope on the kitchen table addressed to me. It's from UH.

OMG!

OMG!

OMG!

She kept prompting me to open it, but I'm suddenly aware of the butterflies flittering around my stomach.

"Go ahead! It's a thick envelope. That's gotta be good news," she exclaimed.

So, I sat down, fumbled with the seal, and tore into it. I pulled out a fancy letter that read, "Congratulations, you have been accepted…" along with a green UH tee-shirt. And, it's my size!

Rose squealed, "I knew it! I knew you could do it! Congratulations!"

She squeezed me so tight, I think I turned fifty shades of pink. Then, she grabbed the tee, threw it in the wash, and called everyone we know.

We're going out to dinner to celebrate. My choice.

TTYL,

Eva

Dear Kami,

Thankfully my driving lessons *are* slow, and we started in a near empty parking lot. Today marked my fifth lesson.

At one point, I hit the gas instead of the brake and sent us lurching forward. We missed a light pole by mere inches. I gotta hand it to Rose. She calmly said, "It's okay. We've all done it. When you're ready, pull back into the parking space and we'll call it a day." She drove home.

She continued, "You should ask Halee about *her* driving adventures. I won't rat her out, but I *will* say your little incident was minor." And then she let out an awkward belly laugh, which made me laugh.

Ed was already home when we arrived. He took one look at Rose's face and said, "Okay, so what gives?"

She laughed and said, "Mum's the word."

He looked at me with raised brows and replied, "Oh?"

I pulled out a bar stool, sat at the island counter, and hurriedly mumbled, "I almost hit a light pole."

He grinned and said, "Poor Turk," before he started laughing.

Yes! He named his car Turk. In a more serious tone, he said, "I'm glad you're okay, but you *do* know accidents happen, right?"

He passed me a glass of ice water and smirked, "You should ask Halee about her driver training."

Rose interjected and laughed, "I already told her as much, but I think we should let Halee do the telling."

"Okay, okay. I get the hint. I'll ask Halee," as I smiled an unknowing smile. "It couldn't have been *that* bad," I smirked.

Ed laughed, "It wasn't that good either. Just ask her. She'll spill the beans. We can't say we were laughing about it at the time though."

"I'll go call or text her. Then, I'm going to read until dinner if that's okay," I offered.

"Sure. Call her though. It's a great story!" Rose exclaimed.

I called Halee. I was surprised to actually get her because I never know her schedule anymore. Being in graduate school now, she is busier than ever. Plus, she works part time as an intern with a publishing company, so her free time is limited.

Apparently, as the story goes, she and Rose were driving on a two-lane road. It was raining, of course. It's the Pacific Northwest, after all. Halee swears she didn't see the tree laying in the middle of the road and *ran over it*! The oil light started flashing and black exhaust sputtered from the tail pipe. Rose instructed her to turn the engine off and they pushed the car onto the shoulder. Neither of their cell phones had service so they were forced to flag down the first passerby, who thankfully, was a highway patrol officer.

She said that's the one thing she will never live down. Turns out, the entire engine had to be replaced. Insurance covered a portion of it, but Halee said it wasn't cheap.

She couldn't talk long because her break was ending, but her experience, as bad as it was, somehow made me feel more confident. Sad but true.

Going to read now!

TTYL,

Eva

Dear Kami,

Rose swears I've been living in my UH tee shirt. Lol, maybe I have. I should throw it in the wash. I'm excited, what can I say! Excited and a bit nervous.

I just got back from the grocery store. Rose asked me to pick up milk and eggs. This marks my first solo driving experience, and I did fine. I was a little nervous, but it was uneventful, thankfully.

I'm trying my hand at making a casserole for breakfast. I've been helping Rose in the kitchen a lot lately and really like creating yummy meals. Cooking is kind of like art. You can create anything you want. I like that.

My favorite thing to make is soup. And, lemme tell ya . . .I've done my share of experimenting. Most were delicious, but some were simply inedible. I used to love Mama's homemade soup. Always so tasty! Rose makes really great soup too.

I can't believe I'm going to be a college student in four short months! Time flies. Rose says it goes even faster as you get older. Wow!

I'm glad Rose is going with me to help me get settled into my dorm room. She wants to help me run all of the errands and buy the things new college students inevitably end up needing. I am glad she's coming along to help me. I'd probably be too overwhelmed not knowing what's where and who's who. Rose knows the area like the back of her hand, so she will be a huge help.

Apparently, I'm in the older student housing. Rose thought I'd be more comfortable around people my age and older rather than housing with seventeen and eighteen-year old's. I think she's right.

I hope I like my roommate. Her name is Tahari. We've emailed back and forth. She took some time off after high school and is just starting college. She's from Pennsylvania. I'm glad the college sends out emails with our roomie's names and email addresses. It will make actually meeting less awkward since we've already sort-of introduced ourselves.

Like me, Tahari has family who attended UH, her sister and brother. They've both already graduated. Her brother does something for the federal government now and I'm not sure what her sister does. She didn't say.

Tahari is a chemistry major. That's good! Maybe she'll help me with my math classes.

Thinking the casserole is ready. It smells ready!

TTYL,

Eva

Dear Kami,

Rose just left.

She helped me with everything, literally. We ran errands and bought all the things I'll need in my dorm room. She really wanted to meet Tahari, but with the storms on the east coast and in the Midwest, her flight was delayed. She won't arrive until tomorrow.

Hopefully, Tahari will not be picky about her side of the room because I've already unpacked most of my things.

Now, I need to memorize my schedule, figure out what to eat for dinner, and get some ZZZ's.

I'm exhausted! It's like we accomplished a weeks' worth of stuff in a day. I don't know how Rose has so much energy! She has to be tired too. I'll try calling her before I fall asleep. I want to make sure she makes it home safely.

Love,

Eva

Dear Kami,

Well, I'm settling in, Tahari and I are hitting it off, and we're going to our first roof-top barbecue tonight. All the incoming freshman are invited.

We agreed to at least check it out. If it's lame, we'll leave and grab some pizza at a nearby popular spot.

I really lucked out on the roommate front! Tahari is a whirlwind of fun, seriousness, mystery, and darkness crammed into a tiny, size 0, package. She also has the looks.

Her family is middle eastern, not exactly sure from where, but she's rocking the dark hair, dark eyes, and beautiful skin. Kill me now!

She's straight, so it keeps things simple. She considers herself a LGBTQ ally.

One of Tahari's friends are coming to the rooftop extravaganza with us. She's meeting us here around six thirty. I can't remember her name right now. Tahari said she's a few years older and lives off campus. I guess her parents are loaded and bought her a condo. Tahari visited her a year or so ago, in-between jobs, and said she has quite the set-up.

Tahari knows I like to spend time under my bed. She even tried it but said she felt claustrophobic. She didn't think I was weird at all. She thought it seemed cool!

Time to shower! I'm grungy. We stayed up too late watching movies last night and I slept most of the day away. Later!

Love,

Eva

Dear Kami,

The rooftop party was pretty much a bust. If you like lots of noise, crowds, and badly burned food, you would love it. Since I like none of the above, I wasn't impressed. Thankfully, neither was Tahari.

Her friend, Sabry, was a no-show, but later texted and asked if we wanted to stop by. By the time Tahari noticed the text, we were both already in our pajamas and didn't really feel like going anywhere. I scrolled through a few messages on my phone and fell asleep sometime after. I honestly don't know what time that was. I was beat, that's all I know.

But, the next morning, Tahari and I were jolted awake by a police-sounding knock on the door, the kind of knock that makes your stomach feel like it's going to plunge right through your butthole and then through the floor.

It was Sabry! So much for looking decent for a first meeting! My hair was in knots, my eyes were sleepy, and I'm sure drool played a factor *somewhere* on my face.

Sabry greeted us with lattes and bran muffins; both were perfect.

She apologized for bailing on the roof-top party and confessed to having unbridled sex with a total stranger! Yes . . . A stranger! Apparently, she met him on Tinder.

Of course, she filled Tahari in on the details and didn't seem to mind me listening. I tried to listen with my mouth closed because at some point, I realized my mouth was hanging wide open, lol.

I like her so far! She's going to be fun.

I'm liking Hawaii already!

Love,

Eva

Dear Kami,

My classes suck! I got lost trying to find my first class this morning and was late to my afternoon class. The professor didn't check attendance, so I guess it doesn't matter. It sounds like a graduate student is going to be doing more teaching than the professor. I don't care though . .

As long as they teach us what we need to know, I'm all good.

I really hope classes get better because I'm really hating life at the moment.

I've never in my life, seen such huge classes. I'm guessing this is not one of those classes where you really get to know the professor.

I just got off the phone with Rose and Ed. Rose said her first week here blew.

I don't want to deal with a whole week of getting lost and being late. I thought I had my routes mapped out, but apparently, I was wrong. Whoops . . .

Time for dinner,

Eva

Dear Kami,

Classes are getting better. Or, should I say, I'm getting better at finding them. I haven't been late since the first week! Wahoo!

I'm getting better!

It's Friday, and Tahari and I are going to Sabry's house for dinner and drinks. Since we're all going to be drinking, we're staying the night. I promised Rose I wouldn't put myself in any dangerous situations. I intend to keep that promise despite Sabry's interest in sex with total strangers.

We're leaving here around six o'clock. Sabry's excited about us trying a new Pinterest recipe she has been dying to make. She said she doesn't like cooking for herself because she ends up wasting so much. We'll see…

I'm better about eating and trying new things, but some things are a stretch.

Sabry's cousin, Margo, is also going to be there. She's visiting for a while.

Sabry is making grape margaritas. I've never even heard of grape margaritas! I'm not a huge tequila fan, but Tahari said Sabry only uses the good stuff, Patron. I guess I'll suffer through it, lol.

I'm going to grab a shower before Tahari gets back and takes over the bathroom.

Later,

Eva

Dear Kami,

What a weekend! I spent most of yesterday nursing my hangover. Tahari too . . .

I'm glad I have today to get back to normal before classes tomorrow. Tahari's first class of the week is on Tuesday. Lucky her!

Sabry's dinner was amazing! She made a chicken and black bean soup that was to die for! I do love my soup!

And . . . There's Margo!

What planet did she come from? She's so . . . Her . . . IDK . . . Margo-ish.

I've never met anyone like her in my life! We hit it off like I thought would be impossible for two people to do. I mean . . . Wow!

She has the best hair. And skin . . . And eyes . . . And smile . . . She is a perfect mix of Hawaiian and Middle Eastern. I would have never guessed Hawaiian, but she wears it well! She has this beautiful sun-kissed-looking skin. And those eyes... Brown and dreamy.

I'm so pale in comparison.

She kept wanting to touch and look at my skin. I didn't mind at all. I liked it. She said my skin was super soft.

She can touch me anytime she likes, although I didn't actually say that to her.

Oh, and the most interesting thing about her . . .

She sails.

Yes, she does! And, from what she said, she's pretty good at it! She invited me to go out on her boat sometime. She said she would show me the ropes, teach me to sail.

Apparently, her parents bought her the sail boat for her sixteenth birthday. She'll only have it for about a month longer because her parents are buying her a brand new one for her twenty-first birthday, which is coming up soon.

We literally spent the entire night talking and laughing while Tahari and Sabry gossiped about men.

We exchanged numbers and have been texting. I can't wait to see her again!

She invited me over on Wednesday for a moonlight madness celebration.

There will be a full moon, so she said it will be the perfect introduction to sailing. Sailing under a full moon is her favorite time to sail.

I forgot where she said she docks her boat, but I'm sure she'll text me the details later.

She is all I've been thinking about since I first laid eyes on her.

She told me she started sailing at eight-years-old. I can't imagine!

Thinking of eight-year-old Margo throws me into thinking about my childhood. About me at that age. I certainly wasn't sailing boats.

I wonder if the private investigator has any more leads? I know Mama would be so proud of me. I'm not going to ask Rose though. I feel like I ask enough already. Realistically, I know either Rose or Ed will tell me when they hear news about Mama. Doesn't keep me from hoping...

I have no idea where Tahari is. I'm a little hungry, so I think I'll wander around and see if I stumble across anything good.

Love,

Eva

Dear Kami,

My brain will not quit! All my thoughts end up trailing off onto the beautiful woman I just met.

Margo, what have you done to me?

I get to see you again tomorrow! So excited!

Love,

Eva

Dear Kami,

I don't know where to begin.

I mean, I literally had the most perfect evening ever! I wasn't even afraid.

Margo knows I can swim, but am far from being an Olympic swimmer.

As soon as I set foot on the dock, she was there with a life jacket ready to strap me in. She quickly went over her most important rule-to always wear a life vest.

Thankfully, hers are high-tech. They inflate when they hit the water, so they're not in the way on the boat.

And, the best part ... She buckled the vest up for me. I loved watching her petite, skilled hands right in front of me, almost touching, but not.

I rode my yellow scooter Tahari affectionately named 'The Busy Bee' to the Keehi Marine Center off the Sand Island access road.

Margo was waiting for me and was talking with a security guard. He motioned me over to an area where I parked my scooter. He said it would be safe and no one would bother it.

Margo showed me around her boat. She actually lives on it. I didn't know that.

It's a Hunter sailboat and is 35' long. I can't imagine driving anything that long! She named it Charlie. Her new boat is being checked out by a mechanic. It's a 2017 Beneteau. It's also 35' long and only has 43 hours on it, whatever that means.

Enough about the boat!

We talked, walked around the marina, laughed and sailed.

At midnight, we sailed Kaneohe Bay.

She showed me Coconut Island, where the opening of Gilligan's Island was filmed. She also pointed out a sandbar called Ahua Laka which is protected by a huge barrier reef.

I'm in awe! We didn't talk about our sexuality. I don't even know if she likes girls!

Man, I'm going to be a mess until I know more.

Margo, Margo, Margo!!!

Love,

Eva

Dear Kami,

I've crashed and burned. I keep thinking about Margo and her skill. I mean . . . Sailing around Kaneohe Bay that night was like second nature to her.

She seemed confident and never questioned what she should or shouldn't do.

I'm not confident, and question everything.

How could someone with so much beauty and adventure at their fingertips possibly have any interest in me?

Margo *lives* beauty.

She steps off her boat slip into the star-studded darkness onto her own, personal sail boat. What's not to love?

That night, as I recall, we never really talked about our pasts. When she finds out about

Mama, I know she'll run. How difficult would it be for her to pull up stakes and sail away? Or worse, ignore me and stay.

We've been texting, but we've both been busy. I've been busy with classes and she has been busy with some regatta.

Why do I always do this to myself? I over think everything. Literally.

Tahari asked me why I've been spending more time under my bed than normal. I just told her I've been super stressed lately. I didn't want to tell her about my internal dialog. I can't have her thinking I'm cra--cra.

I feel like I need a solid three to four days of nothing but sleep and quiet. This depression, slump, or whatever you want to call it is exhausting! I just want everything to be okay.

GTG,

Eva

Dear Kami,

I got the best phone call ever!

Melissa called to tell me her news. She's pregnant! I can't wait! She asked me to be the god-mother. Of course, I said yes! OMG!!!

She's about three months along. Because she was also adopted and doesn't know about her family history, she is having genetic testing done.

I also told her about Margo. She helped me think through my madness. She always knows what to say!

She's right about one thing for sure. Margo and I *have* been texting. That's positive.

And, Melissa says everyone has history. She said some people may seem like they have everything together but in reality, they don't. She added there are a lucky few who make it through this life unscathed, but not many.

Apparently, I'm one of the most interesting people Melissa has ever met. That's something.

Then, she said if Margo is afraid of my past, it's her loss. I guess she's right. I mean, I am a good person. I try really hard. I just need to keep telling myself that.

Everything else is good.

My classes are okay. Rose was right. The general education classes you have to take blow! They're just boring! I feel like I'm back in high school. I can't wait to get into the art classes and meet the professors!

Things are still great with Tahari. She's a great roomie!

Love,

Eva

Dear Kami,

Tahari said Sabry invited us to go hiking to explore waterfalls this weekend. Tahari already has plans, but Margo texted me and said she's in.

Through the tangled web of snapchat and texting, wires got crossed and Margo and I are now the only ones going. I can't say I'm upset about that, lol.

Margo said she heard about a beautiful hike and asked if I'm okay with that. Of course, I am!

I'm okay with anything Margo-related!

I wonder how Sabry got things so confused? She's a bit of a wreck if you ask me, but at least she's a nice wreck.

I need to find my hiking shoes.

With my luck, they're probably sitting at the bottom of the one box I didn't unpack and crammed into the back of my closet. Time to start searching!

Hoping,

Eva

Dear Kami,

Of course, my hiking shoes were at the very bottom of the box that was under a pile of blankets in my closet.

The box was jam-packed with clothes. I didn't realize I had so many!

I've already put together the perfect hiking outfit! Or, should I say, Tahari put it together for me and asked why I seemed so excited about a hike.

Yes, she guessed it!

She knows. She didn't say much about it. She only smiled a smile that reached from ear to ear. She promised she wouldn't say anything to Sabry. My crushes have a way of not always working out, so I don't want to end up looking like the love-sick puppy if things don't happen the way I've imagined.

Tomorrow is the big hike! I'm going to pack water and snacks for both of us. I just need to find some healthy snacks. I'll see if Tahari wants to walk to the market with me.

GTG,

Eva

Dear Kami,

I'm in la-la land. Happy la-la land . . . Going to nap. Will fill you in later.

Love,

Eva

Dear Kami,

I finally got some sleep! I'm on cloud nine.

I'm definitely a lesbian! If I wasn't sure before, I'm sure now.

Margo and I hiked. And hiked . . .

I mean, we really hiked. I was beat; she is in such great shape, she wasn't gasping for every breath like I was.

Margo is a hiking machine! We veered off the main hiking trail and pushed our way through thick brush for what seemed like forever. Then, we found it! Margo lit up like the brightest sunrise ever when she saw the small, three or four-foot waterfall.

She walked over, quietly sat under the cascading water, extended her hand, and gesture for me to sit next to her.

Somewhere between grasping her hand and taking three steps to reach her side, I tripped. Of course, I tripped. My middle name should be Grace. Instead, I have no middle name. Go figure!

Margo was wearing a light-colored tee-shirt. The water gently and perfectly highlighted her beautiful breasts. I was done-for! Hooked! Her magic wound me up and captured my heart and mind. I was twitter-pated.

And... Suddenly, our eyes locked. My heart was pounding like a jack-hammer breaking up asphalt. Before I knew it, Margo was in my lap, straddling me.

I gasped. Before I could even think about catching my breath, I realized our raspy breath was in-sync.

Margo went for gold! One hand trailed directly up my shirt and single-handedly unbuckled my bra while the other hand trailed over my face. I was already in ecstasy. I could have died at that moment and felt like my life was perfect.

My breath hitched. My breasts felt so free. Both nipples betrayed me and stood totally erect. Normally, I would have been embarrassed, but all I could do was try to breath and hope this moment never ended.

I had to touch her! I forced my trembling hands to either side of her face. I stroked her face and hair. Such beauty!

Margo was furiously working my shorts and almost had them around my knees. I should have been worried about getting caught, but I wasn't.

As soon as her fingers started working their magic, I gasped audibly. Oh, how wonderful!

She removed her fingers, pushed me back, and began kissing and licking me where I could have only hoped she would. I had three orgasms. Not one, not two, but three!

I wanted to return the gesture, but she placed her fingers over my mouth. She suggested we hike out and return to her boat.

So, we did . . .

We made soft, passionate love all night long. She slowed me down a time or two, but other than that, our bodies danced together in between the sheets like we were meant to be.

We didn't do a lot of talking, and man . . . I've never been so tired. But, I've also never been so happy, which, leads to my next thought . . .

Are we an item? We didn't exactly stop to talk about it.

Apparently, I'm not so bad at returning the favor. Margo had a big "O" while I explored with my tongue. She tasted so sweet!

I smelled like Margo until I hesitantly washed her sweetness off my body and face.

Oh, how I want to smell her on my face again! So sweet . . .

I want to text her. I want to tell her how I feel. But, I don't.

Instead, I wait.

I wait and hope, and am not let down.

At 7:45 p.m., I heard my phone ping.

She texted me!

The text read, "Hi E! I loved our hike and hope you did too. I hope I wasn't too rough on ya! I'd love to do it again! I'm pretty busy this week, but I'm open this weekend." -M

And, that's all it said. I guess that's better than nothing! Here's to waiting and wanting more!

Love,

Eva

Dear Kami,

Margo and I spent the entire weekend together. I left my room on Friday afternoon and just returned in time to study for an exam. I must force myself to study and not think about the weekend!

I would say, "Poor Tahari," I left her all alone . . . But, it seems she was busy while I was away. She met a new beau named Daniel. Apparently, they did a little dancing in-between the sheets also. Tahari said they too, were together all weekend! She seems pretty smitten with the guy. That's good. She deserves to be happy!

Back to my weekend . . . Margo and I talked about everything under the sun. We talked about Mama, Ray, Rose and Ed, and Ki and Halee. We talked about Ian, Melissa, and about her chaotic-sounding family.

Her family drama sounds almost as dysfunctional as mine. She has an older brother she hasn't seen in over ten years. Yes, ten years. His name is Thomas. Apparently, her parents disowned him over his fondness for young girls. He moved to Brazil where his perverted affections will not get him arrested.

And, you have Margo's parents. They're both doctors. Margo said they were never around when she was a child. Her nanny took her to school, cooked for her, etc....

She said her Dad had the big idea to diversify and invest in foreign markets, which eventually led to them almost being arrested for money laundering. She said she has no idea if they really did it or not, but the drama led to her attending not one, but two semesters at sea through the School at Sea program. She said it was her escape from reality and led to her realization that there are some normal people out there.

She said she loved sailing around in her floating classroom. She loved the Nautical

Science program. She said they spent a little time in a lot of countries, so she was able to see a lot in a short period of time. This is where she really gained a more in-depth understanding of sail theory, passage planning, and navigation.

Apparently, her parents made and invested so much money, after the money-laundering near-miss, they pulled up stakes and fled the country legally. They both work for Doctors Without Borders now. She said she sees them once or twice a year. She's usually the one to sail or fly to whatever country they happen to be working in.

So, she's not afraid of my past. She said she likes challenges, lol.

I had to laugh when she said that because even the slightest memory of things-past makes me happy to have moved-on.

Whew, talk about challenging! I was certainly that! Thank God for Melissa!

Margo and I really hit it off! I mean, like, really, really, really well.

She looks so normal from the outside. You'd never guess she has a pedophile for a brother or parents who almost ended up in prison. I guess looks really are deceiving.

She also says I look totally normal though. Huge ROTFLMAO to that one!

Must study,

Eva

Dear Kami,

Margo and I have been spending every possible second together. When we aren't together, we face time a lot.

I'm realizing I really love being around her. I feel much more grounded when we're together. Kind-of the same feeling I get around Melissa.

She wants me to meet her parents! They are both flying in to inspect her new boat upon its arrival. She wants me to be there with her. She said she feels more confident when I'm around. IDK how a girl who sails around the world by herself ever lacks confidence, but ... The gesture makes me feel good, anyway.

I think I would normally be nervous about meeting someone's parents, but I'm not for some reason. Maybe it's the whole money-laundering thing? Whatever the reason, I'm glad to be meeting them.

I am nervous about seeing the new boat for the first time though. We've made so many memories on the old one already. She wants me to name the new one. I told her I like the names Sam and Ida. I had a great grandmother named Ida and a great uncle named Sam according to Mama.

Margo didn't seem too keen on the name Ida, but didn't seem to object too much when I mentioned the name Sam.

She said I had to see the boat in person before I could officially name it. Makes sense, I guess. I mean, would you name a puppy before you met it? Probably not.

TTYL,

Eva

Dear Kami,

Sam, it is! Margo's new boat is definitely a Sam! And, she agrees, which is the best part. She's going to have the name painted on it soon, which makes my permanence visible. The boat will forever be known as Sam--a name I gave it.

The name of the boat is the easy part. Now, to the not so easy stuff . . .

Margo wants me to take a semester off to go sailing with her. She wants us both to charter Sam's first big voyage. Rose and Ed will certainly be concerned. I have no idea how to break the news to them.

I mean, I really want to go with her. I can't imagine not seeing her for months on end. And, the adventure sounds amazing!

I've had butterflies in my stomach since she mentioned it. I think I should break the news to Rose and Ed in person. I'm sure they would feel more comfortable if they met Margo.

Uggg . . . This adds another level of craziness to my world. Not only do I need to tell them about taking a semester off, I need to introduce them to Margo. I told them about her months ago. They keep asking when they're going to meet her. So, I guess soon will be as good a time as any.

When I asked Margo if she felt nervous at all about meeting Rose and Ed, she half-laughed. You know, that kind of half-laugh that exudes a crude confidence . . .

I get it though. When you've been through a certain amount of life-changing stuff, it can take an earthquake to really rattle you to the core.

Meeting her parents was a breeze. Literally. They weren't even like typical parents. They were more like twenty-something friends. She said that's the way they've always been. Like twenty-something-year-old friends who try to buy friendship and affection. Sad really…

But, at least she's getting a really cool boat out of it! The only thing twenty-something about my Mama is her love of illicit drugs, and not in a good way.

Well, I better start thinking about how I'm going to break the news to Rose and Ed.

Kill me now,

Eva

Dear Kami

Margo is flying home with me over the Christmas break. Everyone is super excited about meeting her. Ki is also bringing someone. She has been dating a guy named Tim Duncan (yes, he has two first names). She's bring him for everyone to meet. As far as I know, Halee is coming alone. She's probably too busy for a relationship anyway. She's pretty relationship wary after the tool she dated in high school. I guess he cheated on her more than once. Poor Halee! She has such bad luck with men.

Melissa and Justen will also meet Margo. They're coming over for Christmas dinner. Melissa is over the moon excited to meet her! Of course, she is though . . . She's Melissa!

Getting a little hungry,

Eva

Dear Kami,

So, Margo and I have been planning our sailing adventure. We want to explore Samoa's big island, Savai'i. She has been there before, and loves it. She said it's a great place to get a feel for the traditional Samoan way of life. She also said the hikes around the island are beautiful.

From there, she wants to visit the Cook Islands. She said one is known as the Island of Pearls. Rose loves black pearls, so I know I won't be able to leave without at least a few for her. We'll also sail to the Great Barrier Island, Pueu, Tahiti, and then back to Hawaii.

Margo knows I'm a little scared, but she promises the places we're going are safe. She also promises we won't take any risky chances under sail.

I trust Margo with my life, so down deep, I know we'll be fine. I still worry though. That's just what I do!

Love,

Eva

Dear Kami,

Christmas at home was magical! Rose and Ed put up four huge Christmas trees, lined the staircase with lights, and had ornaments with Ki, Halee, and my picture displayed on each tree.

I have the perfect family for me!

Everyone loves Margo! Including me.

On Christmas morning, I chanced an "I love you." Margo smiled warmly, kissed me, and said she has loved me since the first time she saw me.

I melted.

Just as I figured, Rose was worried about our sailing adventure. But, she also said this sounds like the adventure of a lifetime and just wants us to be safe. She listened to Margo's every word and seemed comforted by her knowledge. Ed couldn't resist showing off his limited nautical knowledge and volleyed stories back and forth with Margo.

Even with all my news, Halee stole the show. She's dating a guy named Max. They're pretty serious. And, she brought him with her! They spent most of their time with us, but also went to visit his family. He's an engineer, and a super brainiac to boot. I really like him. He seems to treat her well.

And, there's Ki and Tim. Those two couldn't be better matched! I see a wedding coming up in their future. They've even discussed having kids. That works for me because I want nieces and nephews!

With everyone still in the living room, Ed handed me a rectangular shaped box and told me to go ahead and unwrap it. Margo was smiling, so I knew she was *in* on the gift.

I tore the wrapping paper open, took the lid off the box, and saw the folded papers. Once I realized what it was, I cried at least a coffee cup full of tears. Okay, maybe that's a bit much, but I cried, and cried, and cried.

Margo put her arm around me and I let out a belch of sobs. Rose and Melissa joined in on the crying party. Finally, the voice of calm spoke up and said, "Eva, what do you think? Are you okay with this?"

Once I gained my composure, I took a better look at the paperwork and realized just how much my family loves me. They found Mama! And, they found a six-month residential drug treatment program for her. Melissa actually found the program, but Rose and Ed are paying for it.

The other news . . . They actually met her! The private investigator put Mama up in a hotel, so she could get cleaned up and have a safe place to sleep for a night or two. Rose and Ed brought along copies of pictures of me and flew out to San Antonio, Texas to meet Mama.

Turns out, she has been in rehab for a month already. She and I have a phone call scheduled in two weeks. Residents of the program aren't allowed outside contact for the first six weeks because of the difficult adjustment period most residents undergo.

I get to talk to Mama in two weeks! I'm a bundle of emotion. I have so much to say to her.

Rose quickly stepped in and said, "We know you'll want to see your Mom, but she made it clear that she wants to have dental work done before you see her. We told her you wouldn't care what she looked like, but she insisted. She's pretty embarrassed about her teeth and skin. We've arranged an appointment with a cosmetic dentist and with a dermatologist who does acid peels to reduce facial scarring. She is getting the best medical and mental health care available."

"Does she know you adopted me?" I asked.

Rose smiled, looked at me, and said, "She knows we love you. That's all she knows."

I know she will love them for loving me. Rose said the cosmetic procedures will begin in about a month and will continue throughout her rehabilitation. I guess both things require several visits and applications.

"So, does this mean I won't actually see her until she finishes the program?" I asked.

"It does, but it also means she may look more like you remember her once these things are done," replied Rose.

And, that was my Christmas!

My life is so full right now! I can't wait to see Mama. The timing is perfect because that should be about the time Margo and I return from our adventure.

Love my Life,

Eva

Dear Kami,

I'm feeling overwhelmed!

There's so much good happening in my life right now. Yes, it's all good stuff, but it's still overwhelming!

Of course, I'm under my bed and in my safe space. Tahari is lying on my bed talking and contemplating what she's going to do without me. I know what she's going to do. Or, should I say I know *who* she's going to do-Daniel, lol . . . I'm glad she has him.

I know I want Mama to know I love her, that I never stopped thinking about her, and that I am looking forward to spending time with her.

I also want to know what she has been up to for the past ten years, but that part can wait. I guess we have forever to talk about that.

I'm sure she'll have things she doesn't want to talk about, just like I do. And, that's fine. I'm just so happy she's safe.

About to snooze,

Eva

Dear Kami,

I want to write down my conversation with Mama, so I never forget it. So, here goes . . .

Hello . . .

Eva, is that really you?

Yes, yes Mama! It's really me. Oh, Mama! I love you so much!

My Princess . . . You've always been my little Princess, but I guess you're not so little anymore. I missed ya so much. There's so much I want ta say ta ya. I met the Paxton's. They seem like real good people. Enough small talk. Tell me about ya. Please.

Once I cleared my throat, wiped my eyes, and got my sniffles out of the way, I began.

I--I don't really know where to start. I--I was in foster care for a while. Some homes were better than others. Rose and Ed adopted me. They have two biological kids, Ki and Halee. They're a really nice family. I couldn't have gotten any luckier. They really love me (I could hear

Mama sniffling in the background). I love them too. I never stopped loving you and hoping I would see you again. My life hasn't been easy, but it's perfect now that you're back. I graduated from high school. And, I'm in college. I am good, I really am. I never stopped learning, just like you taught me.

There was a very brief pause. I heard Mama blow her nose and clear her throat again.

I'm happy for ya. I'm glad ya found a soft spot in this world. I never wanted ya ta end up like me, but then again, I shoulda known ya wouldn't. Ya were always smart-way smarter than me. Too smart ta end up with some dirt-bag like Ray. I'm so sorry my Princess. Can ya ever forgive me? I understand if ya can't.

There's nothing to forgive, Mama. I know you did the best you could. I'm not angry. I used to be, but I'm not anymore. I'm just glad you're okay.

Brief pause . . .

So, you're a high school graduate?

Yeah. I'm in college too. I have a roommate. Her name is Tahari.

I always knew ya was smart! I'm proud of ya, my Princess! The phone monitors just told me

I have a minute and a half left. I just want ta tell ya how much I love ya and I can't wait ta hug ya. This time will go by fast. I'd like ta get outta here now, but God knows, I need the help. I love ya baby girl and I'll see ya soon!

Bye Mama! I love you too!

Tears, tears, tears . . .

Kleenex, Kleenex, Kleenex . . .

And, Margo exhales!

"Thank you for being here with me. I really didn't know how it would go, but I wanted to keep it simple. I'm sorry I didn't tell her about us."

"It's not about us. This is about you reconnecting with your mom. It's important stuff. I know you'll tell her about us when the time is right. And, that's not now. I think it went just the way it was supposed to go. Do you have any idea how proud I am of you? You don't think you're brave, but you are. So brave . . . I love you so much, Eva," Margo lovingly whispered.

And, with that, I was in tears again.

Pass the Kleenex,

Eva

Dear Kami,

We're packed and ready to go. My leave of absence from UH has already been approved and most of my belongings are in storage.

With all the recent news, we decided to change our travel plans a bit. Instead of hitting the Samoan Islands, Cook Islands, New Zealand, and Tahiti, we're just focusing on the Marquese Islands for now. We have all the time in the world to explore the others, but I don't want to miss Mama getting out of rehab or my first god-baby being born.

We're leaving tomorrow, so, we're spending time with Sabry, Tahari, and Daniel tonight. We're all going to Sabry's for dinner.

Everything I'm taking is already on the boat. All that's left for me to do now besides dinner at Sabry's is to call Rose and Ed, Halee, and Ki and say goodbye.

Gonna shower and get ready for dinner,

Eva

Dear Kami,

I promised Rose I'd keep journaling on the trip. Our first day was exhausting! Because you can't sail directly into the wind, you sail off the wind about forty-five degrees to one side and switch sides from time to time. This is called tacking. Because I'm me, I'm worried we may get off course. Because Margo is Margo, she noticed. She reassured me, telling me this is normal, and we'd correct our course when we could.

She wanted to sail as close to the wind as possible, for as long as possible. She was actually hoping for a storm, which would have given wind in a direction other than from the east. Rough stuff!

I tried using the computer to take my mind off things, and it was basically a no-go. I typed with one hand while I held it steady with the other.

Instead of focusing on the technicalities of sailing, we made a comfortable spot to whale watch. We fashioned a tarp to sit under to keep the sun off us. Margo multitasked, and I was busy looking at and taking pictures of whales. I promised Halee I would take tons of pictures. She's a picture whore! She's jealous and wishes she could come along, but life just isn't budging for her right now. She's so busy every second of the day. She said she's tired before she even gets out of bed some days, just thinking about everything she has to do.

Margo and I have had no shortage of beautiful sea creatures to look at. The reefs in Hawaii are beautiful and are teeming with colorful fish. I don't like going down very deep, but Margo enjoys free diving. She can stay down for about three minutes before she has to come back up for air.

Meanwhile, we were winding down for the evening and listening to the waves crash on the bow. We literally had one rail in the water much of the time. Margo warned that she would be up much of the night making sure we were still on course even though she was using auto pilot instead of her normal line on the tiller process.

The lightning is spectacular!

Going to try to sleep,

Eva

Dear Kami,

I think I have cabin fever. I have been trying to find things to do to keep my mind occupied.

I saw tons of birds earlier. Many were gliding on the air wave pushed up by the sails. They were taking a free ride!

I saw two new birds today ... A Laysan Albatross and a Red Footed Booby.

Last night, I was star gazing on the deck and heard noise nearby. I saw a flying fish flopping around and threw him back in the water. I grabbed his wing and gave him a toss. I can't say that has ever happened to me before.

I also tried fishing today. Within thirty minutes, I had a bite, but whatever is was had no plans of letting me bring it on board. It got away.

I did laundry today. Wooohooo!!!

It was piling up, so I hand washed our clothes using Joy detergent and salt water. I rinsed them in salt water, and then again in fresh water. Margo helped me string some lines about on the stern, so I hung the clothes out to dry. I just had to hope the wind would hold and wouldn't litter the ocean with our clothes.

One really cool sight has been the dolphins. They follow the boat and seem to want to play. I love watching them jump in the air and circle the boat. Margo has actually been swimming with them. I'm a bit too afraid to do that. I'll stick to watching them and taking pictures.

We are about two hundred miles from Nuku Hiva, so we should be there in two days. We'll probably arrive during the night and will anchor there. We'll go ashore and deal with customs after we get a few hours of rest.

Going to try fishing again!

Using a larger hook this time,

Eva

Dear Kami,

Well, Neptune gifted us with decent wind and weather making our final leg into Nuku Hiva. We checked in with customs, which was a breeze. It was much easier than I thought it would be.

And, oh my God!

This island looks like it was hand-plucked from the sea by the Gods! Such unspoiled beauty!

We're exploring the main bay of Taiohae today. Margo said we'll eventually sail to Anaho Bay, on the north end of the island. We want to visit as many islands as possible.

We had a bit of a scare today. We were in the middle of love making when we heard someone yelling. Margo went out on the deck to see what was happening. She sighted a boat banging on a rock with no motor and no anchor. The guy said he had one, but dropped it over the side without attaching it to his boat.

Margo tossed the guy a line and hauled him off the rock using a winch.

The boat lurched forward and plunged into our aft pulpit and damaged the satnav antenna. Margo acted quickly and loaded the third anchor into the dinghy. Then, she went over and attached it to the struggling boat. His dinghy sank a few sails ago, apparently. We helped him get settled and finally left him in the capable hands of a boat repair mechanic on the island.

I've had enough adventure for a day. I'll admit, when the guy's boat hit our boat, I began to panic. I was able to focus my thoughts on hot chocolate and a nice crackling fire to stave-off a full-blown panic attack. Thank God!

It was difficult thinking about hot chocolate and fireplaces when much of what we've been eating is yellow fin tuna. IDK . . . Call me strange, but tropical type food and fish, hot chocolate, and fire places just don't go together.

Margo was proud of me though. Lol . . . I was proud of her! I couldn't believe her bravery in helping that stranded boater. But, she thinks I handled myself like a champ.

We're going for a hike!

And, we finally finished our earlier attempt at love making.

TTYL,

Eva

Dear Kami,

I must admit, I didn't expect to see such vast landscape on Nuku Hiva. From high mountains to massive valleys, it boasts some of the neatest roller coaster like roads I've ever seen.

I was surprised to see horses roaming around free.

We visited the Notre Dame Cathedral one day to take in the beautiful statues of saints, stone buildings, and massive wooden doors that almost seem to beckon you inside. The horses seemed to enjoy the cathedral and the attention they got from passers-by.

And, I rode a horse for the first time in my life. We took a horseback riding tour that lasted about an hour and a half. Margo says I'm a natural. She's been riding horses all her life. My favorite thing about riding was the huge Banyan tree we meandered by. It must also be a favorite of the birds in the area because I saw a ton of tropical birds roosting in the tree.

I'll admit I'm glad we brought plenty of fly spray. The bugs are terrible and seem to thrive in the heat and humidity.

Thankfully, about the time I'd get to the point of almost wanting to collapse from exhaustion, we'd inevitably hit a waterfall, beach, or some way to cool down. The waterfalls on the island are to die for!

Keeping the best part for last...

Wait for it...

Yes! We saw wild boar running around all over the island. The pigs were friendly, thankfully. There's lots for them to eat in the area, coconuts, fish, and other vegetation. What a sight!

We're sailing on to another island.

I'll surprise you with the new location!

Love,

Eva

Dear Kami,

We sailed from Nuki Hiva to Eiao, which is about 120 km, or 75 miles. We anchored on the western side at Vaituha Bay. Our first order of business was refilling our fresh water reserve. Natural spring water is piped in from the mountainside. Margo said it's some of the best-tasting water she's ever had.

We spotted wild goats in the distance. We weren't lucky enough to ever get very close to any of them.

We spent the rest of the first day fishing for our dinner. I hooked a Wahoo fish. Margo helped me reel it in after it was good and tired from chasing the lure.

Margo's reason for wanting to explore Eioa was kind of three-fold. She loves it for its remoteness, but she grew-up listening to stories of gold, gems, and jewels hidden on the island. She also wanted to search for ancient tools made by the Tuametaki people, a Marquesan tribe.

Our entire second day was spent hiking, digging, and searching for treasure.

We didn't find any . . .

Now, I'm spent and exhausted. I wanted Margo to share some of the stories she heard growing up. Stories about gold and treasure . . .

Unfortunately, most of her stories involve pirates. We're here alone for God's sake! And, this bay looks like the perfect place for a pirate attack.

Margo said I've watched too much tv.

I'm still scared. I'm going to try to get some sleep. Margo is holding me, so that makes things better.

Later,

Eva

Dear Kami,

We're having a blast! We never found treasure on Eiao. We had so much fun looking for it though. We'll be back. Eiao is a place I can imagine us returning year after year.

Did I just say, "We'll be back?" Man, we have so many plans together! I've never planned so far in advance with anyone before. It feels nice!

Our visit to Tahuata was nice and quiet. We enjoyed the pristine white sandy beaches and wild horses running free and grazing dotted throughout the island.

We free dove for spiny lobsters. Yes, I dove also. They weren't too deep, and the water was super clear. We dove with a fishing net and a stick, so we could move them without getting pinched. We got two! We had lobster and grilled breadfruit for dinner that night. It was to die for!

Hiva Oa Island rocked the beaches! They have white sand, black sand, and pebble beaches. Margo says anywhere you find black sand, you'll find gold. We didn't look for any though. We're going to buy a really nice metal detector to use on our next trip.

Hiva Oa is a sea horse shaped island. Yes, sea horse ... And, it's loaded with papaya and banana trees. I mean, they are everywhere!

We also saw stone tiki statues and petroglyphs out in the middle of the jungle. No rhyme or reason ... It was like a dream. So cool!

Margo said Hiva Oa is where Paul Gauguin lived and died. We visited the Gauguin Museum in Autuona. No wonder I liked the island so much. It's like an artist's gathering place. Many artists have relocated there.

We met a couple on another boat. They are from Hungary. They're both artists--they paint. They loved hearing about my blown glass and admitted they've always wanted to try their hands at it.

We shared travel stories and a wonderful yellowfin tuna dinner complete with papaya and bananas. They were both very sweet, but I doubt we'll see them anymore on this trip, as they are departing for the Mediterranean. I hope they make it through the Red Sea with no problems. Kidnappings are not rare in that area.

Our last island-hop before heading back was Fatu Hiva, which was a bitch. It was a difficult sail, to say the least.

Fatu Hiva is the southernmost island of the Marquesas.

As we sailed into the bay, I was in awe over the mountains. They were so tall, you couldn't see the tops.

The only way onto this island is by boat. There are only less than six hundred people who live here; it's pretty private.

So, when we found inviting waterfalls and swimming holes, we didn't think twice about shucking our clothes. There were wild orchids growing alongside the waterfall, which framed it beautifully. There were wild orchids growing all over the island!

IDK what it was . . .

Maybe it was the water cascading down Margo's beautiful and naked body . . . But, suddenly, I can't help myself. I grab her, push her up against a rock wall, and start kissing her body. I'm not gentle. I'm too turned on to be gentle. Her dark hair contrasting with the colorful orchids makes it even more intense. I drop to my knees, grab her hips, and rock them into my face. Oh my God, she's my heaven on Earth! And, just like that, she moans in absolute ecstasy. And, I'm happy. I've done my job. Again . . .

When we're ready to hike out, we stopped so I could buy a Umuhei, which is kind of like a Hawaiian lei. It incorporates fruit and is said to possess aphrodisiac properties. I can only hope! I'll take more of what I had earlier, any day!

We picked up the best starfruit I've ever had in my life. I ate four of them by myself. Margo just shook her head and smiled.

We're going to catch a nap and I'm hoping the Umuhei works its magic.

Wish me luck,

Eva

Dear Kami,

We're back in Hawaii. Melissa is due to deliver any day, and Mama gets out of rehab in three weeks.

I'm living on the boat with Margo. Tahari and Daniel got married and didn't tell anybody while we were away. IDK why they are being so secretive. They aren't planning on telling her parents anytime soon. They are renting a house together near the campus.

I'm in la-la land today. Margo is teaching a sailing class and I'm being lazy. Oh well, it's my lazy Saturday.

I keep thinking about our sail back to Hawaii. We literally sailed naked the entire way. I felt so free! I miss the vivid moonlight and twinkly-starred southern hemisphere nights. I miss feeling the water splash and spray past the hull. I miss the majesty of the ocean and our simple diet. On land, food is just handed to you. You don't have to work for it. Boring!

But, November is the start of cyclone season in the south Pacific, so we needed to get back well before that.

The only issue we encountered on the return sail is that several strands of a main stroud broke (the wires that hold up the mast). Margo made adjustments to limit stress on the rigging and added ropes to try to save the mast in case the stroud failed.

I think I'm bored. I miss the action and adventure. Margo said that feeling is normal. She said she always gets the post-sail blues. But, she said she also gets the, *What am I thinking* nerves each time she sets out on a lengthy sail because something almost always comes up, no matter how new or old the boat is. She said she has always been pretty lucky, but doesn't pass up opportunities to help other boaters. She believes in karma, so she believes what comes around will go around. Makes sense.

My classes start up again on Monday. My only Monday class is at two o'clock PM, so I'll be able to sleep in.

Later,

Eva

Dear Kami,

I'm a godmother! Melissa and Justen had a beautiful baby girl!

They named her Kami Grace.

The minute I held her in my arms, I knew I loved her! I can't imagine how Melissa and Justen feel. I've never felt such absolute and pure love in my life. How can I love this tiny bundle of joy so much? I'm just meeting her for God's sake! She literally just came into this world and is already loved so much by so many people.

Rose keeps swooning. The day we make her a grandma . . . OMG! Those children will be spoiled!

I can only stay another two days because I have class.

Ki and Halee picked me up from the airport, but Ed and Rose will drop me off when it's time for me to fly out.

I'm still reeling from Melissa kind-of naming her daughter after me. When she gave me the name-speech, she said Kami, even though fictional, helped me overcome more in my short years than most people go through in a lifetime. She chose the middle name Grace because she said she hopes Kami makes her way through life with as much grace as I've shown.

Wow!

I've gone from the weird goth girl who foiled the school shooting plot to Melissa naming her first born with me in heart and mind.

I'm aware of my fondness for Kami Grace and realize I may want children one day. I wonder if Margo has ever thought about having kids? We've never talked about it. We've talked about so much on our adventures, I can't believe that never came up.

Going to make an ice-run for Melissa.

TTYL,

Eva

Dear Kami,

Back in Hawaii!!!

My phone is flooded with pictures of Kami Grace. I used up so much memory, I had to delete a few photos.

And, I'm thinking about Mama. I called her, and we had a nice, long talk today.

Rose and Ed have a dry cabin in their back garden. When Mama gets out of rehab, she'll stay in the cabin for a while. There's no plumbing, but Mama can use the spare bathroom in the garage. It's totally private and nobody ever uses it.

Mama was a little hesitant about it at first, but this way, we can spend quality time catching up while she figures out what she's going to do with her life.

Rose suggested she live in one of their rental houses. One became available as of two weeks ago. The long-time tenant moved to Cambodia. Yes, Cambodia! IDK why.

Rose says the rent is low and it's small enough that maintenance and up keep would be

Idiot

simple. I think it's a fabulous idea. I'll have to try to talk Mama into it, I'm sure.

I'll have to miss classes when she gets out. I've already spoken to my professors and they are good with it. They will give me the assignments before I leave so I won't fall too far behind.

Margo is excited for me! She'll stay in Hawaii when I fly back. Rose and Ed have it set up so I can spend as much alone time with Mama as possible.

Uggg . . . The wind is rocking the boat.

I need a nap,

Eva

Dear Kami,

I flew home in time to pick Mama up with Rose and Ed. When we pulled in, Rose gasped, "She looks so much better! I can't believe how healthy she looks."

And, I bawled . . .

Like a baby . . .

Mama took off running toward me at almost a full run. She snatched me up, bear hugged me, and twirled me around. I couldn't stop sobbing.

Mama looked at me, cupped my face with her hands and cried, "My little Princess! You're not so little anymore. You're beautiful. Oh, my baby… My baby…"

I tried to talk, but could only mumble, "Mama."

She shispered, "Shhh, Princess. It's okay," as we walked to the car.

Rose and Ed got out of the car as we approached and wrapped us both in their arms, in a big group hug.

I couldn't stop bawling. Thankfully, Rose brought a box of Kleenex along for the occasion. She's always so thoughtful. She knew I'd need them.

We drove home and had the best surprise ever. Melissa snuck in while we were picking Mama up and put a huge bouquet of roses in a vase on the table, strung a welcome home banner in the living room area, and placed the best-smelling cookies on a plate beside the flowers.

I can't believe she did that! I have the best family in the whole world!

Rose and Ed left us alone in the cabin and told us dinner would be at 5 p.m.

It took a good hour before I could say anything that wasn't jumbled and made any sense. I was just so overwhelmed by emotion.

Mama and I sat on the couch together. We sat so close. Like we were afraid to let each other go. I couldn't get enough of her being so near. I don't think she could either. She stroked my head and hair. She kept looking at me without speaking. She looked at me deeply, as if she were looking into my soul.

She started, "My Princess, there's so much I want to say. To share…"

I don't know where it came from, but I said, "Shhh… You're here now. That's all that matters. You don't have to talk if you don't want to. We have our whole lives together. I don't need to hear things you're uncomfortable sharing. I know you had some rough years, like I did. You have a second chance, like I have. Everyone has things they don't like talking about. You don't need to tell me everything. The only thing I need from you is love, and for you to never leave me."

And, Mama cried softly.

She said she wanted to step out to smoke. I followed, and I smoked.

"You smoke?" she asked.

"No, I don't. But, I'm smoking now," I replied with a slight laugh.

"You know what I miss? Your soup. Can you make soup for us sometime? Maybe tomorrow? Rose is cooking tonight, but she's planning on letting us do our own thing most of the time."

"I would love ta make soup. We'll need ta go ta the store sometime tomorrow. What kind of soup do ya want?"

"Anything. I just want your soup. Like you used to make."

Mama smiled, "That'd be kitchen sink soup. I'll come up with something good for us. I haven't made soup in a long time, but it's like riding a bike. Ya never forget how ta make it."

At 5:00, we wandered into the main house. Mama admired Rose's flowers and shrubs that lined the path from the cabin to the house.

"Someone has a green thumb," she mused.

As we walked into the kitchen, I realize Rose made Mama's old favorite, parmesan chicken.

"Dinner smells great," she smiled.

Rose and Ed had already placed silverware and napkins on the table, the plates were stacked on the counter, and we all helped ourselves.

We had the best dinner ever!

Love,

Eva

Dear Kami,

Well, Mama is getting settled. She's living in Rose and Ed's rental, has a job as a cashier at Grocery World, and found a narcotics anonymous group she can live with. It's a little further away than the closest meeting to her house, but she said she feels more comfortable with the people there. So, that's something. I hope she keeps going and keeps clean.

She's riding her bike to and fro' right now. She said she doesn't like riding the bus because last time she rode one, someone threw up on her.

Rose and Ed lent her two thousand dollars to buy a car she saw listed for sale in the paper.

She is repaying them as she can, but will aim for two hundred dollars a month. She picks the car up this weekend.

Ed said even though it's an older Volvo, it's a steal because the mileage is relatively low, it has been stored in a garage out of the weather, and the maintenance is spectacular. The original owner passed away and his son couldn't bear to keep it because of the memories.

Hooray for Mama! She seems to be getting the breaks she needs to give her new life a real go.

She knows I need to get back to Hawaii for school, but she's not happy about it. She hasn't said anything, but I can tell.

I talked to Rose about the situation and she said there are many adjustments and new things Mama will need to get comfortable with. She urged me not to let her discomfort dissuade me from returning to U.H.

It's not . . .

Rose also told me about Dr. Rex, the therapist she suggested Mama see in addition to the N.A. meetings. Dr. Rex isn't covered under Mama's health plan, so Rose and Ed are once again, going above and beyond, and agreed to foot the bill.

Rose said she wants Mama to be as healthy as she can possibly be, as she foresees her being a permanent fixture in our lives.

Yes!!! She said our lives.

I have the most awesome family ever!

We had a huge family dinner before I flew back to Hawaii. Mama made minestrone soup, Rose assembled a tray of hors d'oeuvres, and Ed made spaghetti. Ki and Halee weren't able to come, but Melissa and Justen brought Kami Grace and cookies for dessert. I don't know how Melissa has the time to bake cookies *and* take care of Kami Grace.

Kami Grace stole the show, of course.

Mama smiled, winked at me, and said, "Kami Grace is a lovely name."

I donned a huge teeth-bearing-smile and in my best baby-loving voice said, "Yes, it is, and she's such a special girl."

Over dinner, Melissa said, "I bet Margo is going to be beyond the moon happy to see you!"

I smiled and said, "Yes, she will be."

Mama looked perplexed, realized I saw her, and simply smiled.

I jumped in, cleared my throat, and said, "Mama, you haven't met Margo yet, but you will. She's my girlfriend. You'll love her as much as I do!"

Mama smiled, "I'm glad ya have someone ta love ya! I'm sure I'll like her."

I dug my phone out of my jacket pocket, scrolled through my photos, and found my favorite picture of Margo.

"Here's a picture of her," as I showed Mama.

"She's beautiful, Princess," she said.

"I think so too," I smiled.

After dinner and saying my good-bye's, I headed to bed. Rose is taking me to the airport at five o'clock in the morning.

Arrghh! Sooo not a morning person!

Gotta get some rest,

Eva

Dear Kami,

Being back in Hawaii is nice--ish. I just feel like my entire life is back in the PNW. Except for Margo. I love our time together. Even though I was busy helping Mama, I still missed her while I was away. She's happy Mama is getting settled and wants to meet her.

Rose and Ed made this whole thing happen for me. I really don't know where I'd be without them. Literally. I said that to Rose on the way to the airport. Her only reply was, "You do what you can to help those you love."

I'm going to spend all day tomorrow finishing up assignments while Margo teaches sailing lessons. I'm not too far behind. I got some work done while I was home, thanks to Rose for helping me stay on track.

Margo is calling my name.

GTG,

Eva

Dear Kami,

Classes are fine. Boring, but fine.

Margo is okay.

I'm blahhh, and I don't know why. The only new news is that Mama's job at Grocery World fell through. Apparently, the manager over-hired and had to let the newest person go. That was Mama.

She recently had an interview at another grocery store. It's a larger store and pays a little better than Grocery World. I hope she gets the job! She should know soon.

Mama also started counseling with Dr. Rex. She'll see her every two weeks. Rose said Dr. Rex may eventually like me to attend a few of the sessions, but that will be down the road.

I've been talking to Mama on the phone a lot. About every other day . . . I leave messages on the answering machine when she's not there. I just like her to be able to hear my voice. When we actually talk, we never talk long. Mama isn't a big phone talker. She never has been.

I usually call Rose twice a week or so. She's my go-to person when I feel out of sorts like I feel now.

She says I just need to let the blahhh feeling pass. She thinks I've been stressing out about Mama. I know I have been. She suggested I try to have some me time.

So, Margo and I made dinner plans with Tahari, Daniel, and Sabry. Not exactly me time, but it's close enough, I guess.

Sabry is cooking for everyone again. She's making sushi rolls tonight. That will be nice!

Tahari is a great friend and always cheers me up. We're leaving in about two hours.

Going to try to catch a nap,

Eva

Dear Kami,

Mama got the job and started today!

Hooray!!! She loves it! She's making well above minimum wage and has room for advancement. I'm so proud of her!

Dinner at Sabry's was perfect. Almost.

The sushi was to-die-for.

Sabry introduced us to her newest love interest, fling, or whatever they were calling it. His name is Steve, and I doubt I'll ever forget it.

During dinner, someone started pounding on Sabry's front door yelling, "Steve, I know you're in there, you bastard. Come out!"

Daniel spouted, "What the hell?" as Sabry and Steve exchanged uncomfortable glances.

Margo piped up and sarcastically asked, "Are you going to get that?"

"No. The door is locked. She can knock all she wants."

After about ten minutes of crazed door pounding, we heard a car door slam and tires squealing.

Steve grimaced, "Thank God! She's gone. I should go too."

Once he was out the door, Tahari exhaled, "What in the hell was that about?"

Sabry winced, "I met him on a sugar daddy website. We've been seeing each other for about a month."

"So, he's married?" Tahari asked.

"I never asked. He doesn't wear a ring and he has stayed over a few times," replied Sabry.

"Great! He has a stalker girlfriend then," said Daniel.

"I don't know. I don't care. I don't do crazy. Whatever his issue or story is, he can tell it to someone else. I'm done! I don't need crazy bitches banging on my door. I can find another toy. It's a damn shame though because he's a sex god," Sabry said with a half laugh.

"Jesus, Sab! You really need to be careful. Now, the girlfriend, wife, or whatever she is knows where you live," exclaimed Margo.

"I know. I'm going to send him a get lost text now. Then, I'll block his number, so he can't text or call me again," mumbled a more serious Sabry.

"I'll be more careful," she continued.

"Sure, you will," said Margo sarcastically.

And with that, we finished our dinner and drinks.

That was my evening.

Never boring,

Eva

Dear Kami,

I told Rose about Sabry's dinner party. She's concerned. She thinks Sabry may not be the most stable or suitable friend.

She asked, "Do you know what else she may be into? If she's looking for sugar daddies, who knows what else she may be okay with. I just want you to be careful."

I know Rose loves me and is trying to keep me safe. I really like Sabry though. It doesn't really matter to me who she has sex with. Rose had a good point, I'll admit it. She asked, "What if the woman at the door had a gun and decided to use it? People do crazy things in the heat of passion. Please just promise you'll be careful."

I guess it really doesn't matter because Margo was beyond mad. She never wants to go back over there. She said Sabry can come to the boat or we can meet her out somewhere next time we make plans with her.

And, Mama is doing great. After a few short days on the job, the manager told Mama about an assistant manager trainee position and encouraged her to apply.

Life's a roller coaster,

Eva

Dear Kami,

Rose thinks Mama may be talking to Dr. Rex about the assistant manager trainee program.

Rose explained, "Chronic low-self-esteem is a difficult circumstance to overcome. I hope Dr. Rex is able to help your Mama make the best decision for her. Of course, we believe it's in her best interest to take the promotion and start moving up in her career. But, she may not be ready. We'll just have to wait it out and see what she decides to do."

I know it would be hard for her to step into a position of authority. I don't even know what her life after me was really like, after all. I don't know if she ended up with another man who also beat her. I'll just try to be patient. It's not like there's anything I can do about it anyway.

Rose reminded me that life is about taking steps. Much like the steps I took learning to swim, getting my license, and taking art classes in the community.

She says Mama will come into her own being, at her own pace, and we shouldn't rush or try to manipulate it. I get it. I really do. I just want the best for her.

Margo is still fuming mad at Sabry. She said her mom's side of the family has always been a bit on the crazy side. Sabry is her second cousin, I believe.

Sabry called Margo yesterday to apologize about the fiasco. She wanted us to go to her house for dinner again, and Margo angrily refused. I must be honest, I've never seen Margo so angry. Sabry finally gave in and agreed to meet at a restaurant, but later texted and cancelled.

I'm not sure what's going on with Margo. She has been angry and distant since Sabry's dinner party. She hasn't offered to talk much about it.

Rose suggested I give her time and let her deal with the situation in her own way.

She gave me some interesting insight though. She said since Margo's parents aren't a real source of stability or safety for her, she may seek those things from others. When Sabry's actions didn't match Margo's ideal, it forced her to react. Fight or flight. Margo seems to be great at the flight part, and *not* fighting keeps her safe.

I'm trying to be patient with Mama and Margo.

I don't like being patient,

Eva

Dear Kami,

This morning, after we woke, Margo asked if we could meet around lunch time to talk.

I stared into space and doodled in my notebook during my mid-morning class. I just couldn't get into it. My thoughts were solely focused on Margo and on what she could possibly want to talk about.

She has been distant lately.

Arrghhh! My stomach is in knots.

FML,

Eva

Dear Kami,

I'm with Daniel and Tahari. Tahari hasn't left my side since she heard the news yesterday.

The nurse just came in and said the doctor is completing my discharge paperwork.

According to Tahari, Rose is on her way and should be landing at Honolulu International soon. She is renting a car at the airport.

I'm woozy from the meds.

TTYL,

Eva

Dear Kami,

Rose booked a hotel room not too far from Tahari's place. I'm going to stay with her for a few days until we figure things out.

Tahari checked for me, and Sam has set sail. Margo is gone!

When we had our talk, Margo said she was going to head out and didn't know where she was going. She said she just needed to get back out on the water. She said she would be back, but had no idea when.

I asked if she wanted me to come along, and she said she wanted to sail this one alone.

If there's one thing I understand, it's rejection. I know it well. I don't think she'll be back. If she comes back, it won't be for long, and it won't be for me.

Ray used to call me Idiot. But, I'm nobody's idiot, I can tell you that for sure!

She wouldn't really go into details with me. I told her I would miss her, and she spoke to me like a child. She didn't say she would miss me.

And, it happened . . .

I couldn't breathe; my throat was closing. I was shaking, sweating, and my heart was beating so hard and fast I thought I was having a heart attack. The chest pain was excruciating.

Margo tried calming me down, but I went from really bad to worse. I was dizzy, light headed, and was afraid I would faint.

Margo called Tahari, who left class and rushed over. She drove like a bat out of hell and took me straight to the emergency room. By the time we arrived, I was distraught. The ER admission staff ushered me straight back because they also wanted to rule out a heart attack.

Tahari spoke with the ER doctor and told him I had a history of having panic attacks.

While the doctor was checking me over, Tahari called Rose and Ed. Rose booked the first flight out.

The doctor gave me anti-anxiety medicine which made me feel even more depressed when I finally woke up.

Sometime during the interview process, I told the doctor I didn't want to be here anymore. He decided to keep me overnight for observation despite me saying I wasn't planning to kill myself.

Apparently, Margo left my belongings with the security guard where she used to dock Sam. Daniel picked up my things.

I don't know what I'm going to do without her! She's such a huge part of my life. How could she do this to me? To us?

Every time I try to talk to Rose, I cry. She wants me to keep journaling. I just want to sleep.

Here's to sleep,

Eva

Dear Kami,

Well, I slept!

I slept for about fifteen hours straight! I woke to Rose sitting next to me on the bed, softly stroking my hair.

She offered me a bottle of water and I drank the whole thing in a few gulps.

Rose asked if I wanted to get something to eat, and I said, "No."

Finally, she whispered, "Sweet baby girl, you have to eat. I'll call Tahari and ask her to come over for a while. I'm going to find some chicken noodle soup. If I have to, I'll make some."

And, in a split second, Tahari was knocking on the hotel room door.

She ran a bath for me and sat in the bathroom while I bathed. The warm water felt nice, but suddenly I started feeling an aching lonely feeling.

Tahari helped me out of the bathtub, into clean pajamas, and back to bed.

What would I do without Tahari and Daniel?

This pain-staking vulnerability swept over me like a heavy black cloud.

"Will this ever get easier? Will it ever quit hurting?" I asked.

"It will get easier. Eventually. I'm so sorry this is happening, Eva. Is there anything I can get you?" Tahari asked.

"I think I just need to go to sleep. It's the only way I feel any peace. Please don't leave me alone. I don't want to be alone," I begged.

"I'll stay here as long as you need me to," she promised.

About forty-five minutes later, Rose was back with chicken noodle soup. I ate some of it. My body aches all over. My teeth even hurt. I feel like I got run over by a huge truck.

I need more sleep,

Eva

Dear Kami,

When I woke again, Tahari was gone.

"Tahari went home for a while. She'll be back later," said Rose softly.

She continued, "Ed and I want you to come home with us for a while. We think it will be good for you. I mentioned it to Tahari, and she said although she'd miss you, she also thinks it's a good idea. That way, we can get you hooked back up with Dr. Lydia. For what it's worth, Melissa is also on-board."

My head started spinning and I felt dizzy. Rose grabbed the brown paper sack she brought the soup in, and I started breathing into it.

Finally, I'm breathing normally, and the dizziness went away.

"There's no hurry. You don't have to make a decision right now," said Rose.

"That's why I think it would be best if you came home for a while. You have a built-in support system there already. I'm sure your Mama would love having you around too," she said.

"Does Mama know about this?" I asked

"No, she doesn't. We thought it would be best to let you tell her on your own time."

"Thank you," I mumbled and started crying again.

The thought of leaving Hawaii, the very place I've grown to love, and the place I met Margo, overwhelms me with sadness.

"Can we go for a drive? I need to get out of this room for a while," I suggest.

"That's a great idea. We'll go for a drive around the island."

And, we're off,

Eva

Dear Kami,

I've been home for about two weeks now. I feel better, but I still get overwhelmed by this feeling of horrible sadness.

I've seen Dr. Lydia once since I've been home. She says first loves are always the hardest to work through. She says you never forget a first love. She asked me to start thinking about what I learned from my relationship with Margo. She wants me to think about what I liked about her as a person, and what I disliked.

I told her I loved everything about her. She said I may feel like that now, but as time pushes forward, I'd gain new clarity into the situation.

I've never really thought about things I don't like about her. I doubt there's anything I don't like.

Mama's calling,

Eva

Dear Kami,

Mama loves her new assistant manager job. She said the only thing she even dislikes a little is making the schedule.

During lunch, we were interrupted by a man who brought us two free hot teas. I knew something was up with these two!!!

So, I asked, "Ummm, what's going on here?" I was sure Mama was smitten!

She whispered, "He's my sponsor. Ya know, NA sponsor."

I shuffled uncomfortably and whispered, "Oh, I thought…"

"I know what you thought," she interrupted.

"At this stage, a relationship is the last thing I need. My focuses are on ya, staying clean, and keeping my job. Period," she continued.

"Yeah. I'm sorry. I shouldn't have assumed. That was stupid of me," I said.

"Don't be sorry. He's gay. He'll be a catch for a handsome somebody, but not for me," Mama laughed.

We laughed the moment off and finished our lunch. Mama still hasn't asked me one word about Margo. She and Rose must have spoken about it. They're becoming quite good friends. Mama taught Rose how to make her version of Minestrone. They seem to like each other just enough for the situation to be tolerable. Which is good . . .

Mama cleared her throat and said, "Princess, Rose and me . . . We've been talking. She has a friend with an art studio who wants ta expand. Her friend is inta clay, but wants ta maybe see if ya want ta try making your glass in her shop. Rose and me . . . We think it would be a good start for ya."

Clearly, Mama has no real input, but Rose is always trying to at least make other people feel good about themselves. She's special like that.

It's sweet that Mama is trying. It makes my heart feel some twinge of joy.

I smile and say, "That sounds wonderful. I'd like to meet her."

I knew Mama had no idea who the lady was, so I didn't press the issue.

"Mama, I need to get back. I have a dental appointment I have to get to. It's just a cleaning, but I don't want to be late," I said.

We hugged and said our goodbyes.

I thanked Jeff for the tea.

Later,

Eva

Dear Kami,

I met Jewel, Rose's friend with the art studio. She's very hippy-dippy. I like her! She seems to like me too. We really hit it off over coffee.

She wants to continue throwing clay but wants to include the glass aspect too. She said she has gotten four calls in the last few months with people asking if we can incorporate ashes into jewelry or art. I guess when people are cremated, it's actually *a thing* to spin some of the ash into an object. I could get into that for sure. It would be such an artistic way to memorialize someone you love!

She has a huge empty area in her warehouse-looking building. It would make a perfect glass studio. Rose and Ed have already said they would like to make a small investment in my future. I'm guessing that means they want to help buy the equipment I'll need.

Rose suggested a ten percent repayment schedule. So, basically, I'd repay she and Ed ten percent of whatever sells. Seems like a great idea to me!

I'd give Jewel twenty percent of anything I sell as my contribution toward the rent. A total of thirty percent coming out isn't bad at all. It really isn't.

Our little town is a tourist hot-spot in the spring and summer. Jewel said I should consider giving glass-blowing classes during the busy tourist months. The participants could make a vase or ornament that could be mailed to them once it was processed and wrapped.

Rose already got me enrolled in the local community college. I think she's right. Knocking out the general-ed classes at the junior college will be the best way to get them done. Then, when I'm ready, I can focus on upper division classes at my leisure.

I feel like I'm in auto-pilot mode. Everything is just okay. Nothing is perfect or awe-inspiring.

Rose said things may seem like that for a while and that's okay. She said it's my brain trying to cope with loss and moving on. She said it's kind of like a fake-it-till-you-make-it scenario except I'm not faking anything. Supposedly, I'll eventually fall into the rhythm of life and will one-day wake to a new and improved me.

Yes, I get how overcoming something can make you stronger. I just wish my overcoming days were done. They're not though.

I'm better. Yes, I'm better. I still spend much of my days thinking about my time with Margo. My dreams always land on her.

One day, I'll have peace. It isn't in my cards yet though.

Love,

Eva

Dear Kami,

Dr. Lydia suggested I write Margo a letter. A letter I'll never send.

She wants me to tell her how I feel about her actions. She thinks it will help give me closure. Rose, Ed, and Mama agree we should have a big marshmallow roast when I finish it. It can be added as fuel for the fire!

So, here goes . . . . . .

Dear Margo,

I really don't know where to begin. I don't know why you made the decision you made. I really don't. We were doing so well, or, so I thought.

We were building a life together, for God's sake. Or, should I say, I was building a life with you?

You were my first true love. You were my first of a lot of things. My first female lover, my first big "O," my first overnight sailing adventure, my first time living on a boat, my first time searching for treasure on a remote island, and my first major heart break.

You left me broken. I have a broken soul, but am slowly healing.

I left Hawaii because of you. It's not all bad though. I'm now a partner in an art gallery. Yes, I miss Tahari and Daniel. The good thing about it is we facetime, skype, and will visit. Tahari can't wait to see the studio. I can't wait to show her.

I'll never get a chance to show you. I know you won't, but even if you tried to come back, I wouldn't let you. I couldn't stand losing you twice. Losing you once was hell enough.

I keep racking my brain trying to figure out what went wrong or at least where *I* went wrong.

And, I keep coming up empty.

The only thing I come back to is the fact that you've been so independent for so long. You aren't truly close to anyone that I know of. The only things you really truly love deeply are the sea, and your ability to escape when needed (Sam).

You're like a succubus. You suck bits of life out of the people around you. You don't care that I named your boat Sam, after a relative I've never met.

You don't really care about the oat milk you smugly order in cafés and then get all indignant when they don't have it. That too, is another thing you stole. From Sabry. She truly loves oat milk and even makes her own.

There are so many other examples I could list, but I'd be doing myself more harm than good by focusing on them.

I don't think you ever really loved me.

I think you loved the idea of me. Someone real, someone fragile, someone eager, someone impressionable . . .

When I didn't crumble at sea during our hairy adventures, you realized I'm not quite as fragile as you assumed.

When I flew back home without you, you knew I wasn't as fragile as you hoped.

And, when Sabry's uninvited dinner guest raised a ruckus, I didn't even wince. You knew at that moment, I wasn't the fragile flower you hoped I'd be.

So, you decided you would try to destroy me. You wanted me to fall to my knees and shatter.

I'll never shatter! You will not destroy me.

I think your brother touched you in a very bad way. I don't think you've ever told anyone. I don't think you ever will.

I scared you.

I scared you because I'm dealing with the shit in my life that has fucked me up. I want to deal with it. It makes me a stronger person.

You . . . You can't. When things get difficult, you shut them out. Or, you leave completely.

You ripped my heart out and cut it up into tiny pieces. I'm getting better though.

I want to love again. I will love again.

I have a lot to give and a lot to share. I'm not ready right now, but I will be one day. And, I can't wait to meet her.

Yes, it still hurts. It does . . . I need to thank you for being my first of so many things. Because of you, I'm braver. How many people can say they've sailed the open seas and explored uninhabited islands?

I can!

--Eva

Here's to our family marshmallow roast!!!

www.ingramcontent.com/pod-product-compliance
Lightning Source LLC
Chambersburg PA
CBHW071457170626
46811CB00007B/2605